AUGUST ICE

AUGUST ICE

DEV BENTHAM

www.devbentham.com

Published by
Love is a Light Press
POB 685, Minocqua, WI 54548
www.devbentham.com

This e-book is a work of fiction. McMurdo Station in Antarctica is a real place but the author has never been there so it may be entirely misrepresented. Also, any resemblance to actual persons, living or dead is entirely coincidental.

Warning: sexual content. This book contains graphic imagery of men having sex together. And enjoying it. However, the story is primarily a romance. Don't be disappointed if you read pages and pages and pages with-out encountering acts, organs or orgasms.

Dedication

For LJ

who is always willing to dive deep with me

Acknowledgments

Antarctica is a beautiful and challenging setting for a story. Fortunately for me, many people (too many to name) have posted their memories, videos, and pictures online. I'm grateful for all their assistance, and I encourage anyone interested in Antarctica to search out the videos and experience it themselves.

I am truly blessed that Jordan Castillo Price created this exquisite cover for the author edition of August Ice. I am also indebted to her for phenomenally insightful advice on both character and story development in both the earlier version of this story and this current edition. Laurie Cheeley brought to this version her wonderful editorial suggestions and an eye for detail for which I am deeply grateful. I'm also extremely grateful to my editor at Loose Id, Larke Butler, who made the editing of the early version useful, educational, and fun and pushed me to go deeper into the story in every way.

For me this novel, like all recovery stories, is about the possibility of redemption. Most of us fight our own self-destructive inclinations, whether they're active addictions or unhealthy habits. Max is so obsessed with avoiding his past that he almost misses out on his future. Fortunately, he catches himself in time and finds a way to haul himself up from the depths.

Part One

WinFly

"Winter-overs tend to think that WinFly people are loud, pushy and belittling, while folks that arrive at WinFly tend to see the winter-overs as tired, irascible and even slightly paranoid. Winter-overs don't always get the slack they deserve."

Dictionary of Antarctic Slang, Ethan Dicks

http://penguincentral.com/MCMslang.html

Chapter One

Deep blue in all directions. Light streamed in pale shafts from the ice ceiling to the ocean bottom, which burned with deep red sea anemones. A flock of penguins swam close, their sleek black backs brushing against him like a lover. He was swimming with them, pressed by slick feathers on all sides, no tank, no regulator, no cold. Like flying.

* * *

Somewhere a door slammed.

Max Conway squinted one eye open, then shut it tight against the stab of light. He wasn't underwater. Wasn't even in Antarctica. Not yet. He lurched to sitting, and pain rolled through his head like a bowling ball. His mouth felt like he'd been eating mothballs, and his stomach twisted painfully. God, he hated mornings.

He swung his legs off the bed and willed his eyes open a crack. No wonder his head hurt. Someone had left the curtains open. Max could see through to the hotel pool sparkling in the sunshine. Pool? Hotel? He closed his eyes again and tried to reconstruct the night.

The last thing he remembered was doing shots with the guys at some dive bar Bones had found in the eastern suburbs. He sneaked a peak at the room. Beige carpet, a red-and-gold-striped bedspread, a carving on the wall that looked vaguely Maori—typical Christchurch hotel fare. The question was, how did he get here?

"Ah, you're awake." A man's voice, sounding deep, soft with a trace of an accent. Max turned toward the sound, trying to ignore the lurch of his gut at the movement.

A tall, thin man stood at the end of the bed, toweling dry a mop of dark hair and watching him through startlingly blue eyes. He had a classic swimmer's body—strong-chested and slim-hipped—unlike Max's own diver form, packed thick with bulging muscles earned swinging around fifty-pound dive tanks. Lean ropes of muscle ran down The Guy's arms. A tattoo of inky spikes that looked like loops of barbed wire encircled one biceps. Ringlets of hair curled around his nipples and trailed down his belly. A pair of worn blue sweatpants rode low on his hips.

Max licked his lips. It was hard to believe he wouldn't remember having some of that. His gaze traveled back up The Guy's torso to settle in those Antarctic Ocean–blue eyes.

He cleared his throat and managed to croak out, "Hey."

The Guy gestured toward the bedside table. "There's water. You feel terrible, yes?"

Max started to nod and stopped at the vertigo. He turned, expecting to see one of those weenie hotel glasses, but instead, there sat a large red aluminum water bottle.

"Thanks." The water tasted sweet. Max chugged it and waited while the wave of dizziness washed over him. What was it Bones called this, the morning freebie drunk?

Bones. Christ. Had the guys seen him leave the bar with a man? How the fuck would he explain that?

The Guy was watching him. "I'm assuming you don't want breakfast."

Max's stomach rebelled at the thought. He shook his head slowly.

"You're welcome to shower. I'll go to the lobby and get us some coffee." He tossed his towel onto a chair and reached for a sweatshirt.

Max watched him smoothly shove his arms into the shirtsleeves, his torso disappearing beneath the bulky shirt. His head popped through the neck hole, hair already springing into curls. He caught Max watching him, and his lips twisted into a sardonic smile.

Max stood, let his body adjust to the change, and stumbled toward the bathroom. He made the mistake of looking in the mirror. He brushed a hand through his close-cropped brown hair. His eyes, usually his best feature, were so bloodshot they looked more red than brown. Tawny, that was what a guy in California had called them. Max snorted. Right now, they looked more like bloody shit. He turned on the water and stepped out of his boxers. Boxers. And he wasn't sore anywhere. Maybe nothing had happened. Good. He hated to think he'd finally gotten lucky in Christchurch and couldn't remember a thing. And that long, tall drink of whatever was something he was sure he'd hate to forget.

He turned the faucet to as hot as he could stand and stepped in. Jets of water stung his chest. The cascade of warmth felt good, not like that pathetic excuse for a shower at the place he'd been sharing with the guys for the last month while they trained and waited on the weather. He ran a hand over the stiff bristle of stubble on his chin. No razor, no toothbrush, and he felt like shit. Hooyah. He plunged his head into the spray, filled his mouth with hot water, swished it around to dislodge the sweaters on his teeth, and spit. The hotel soap was tiny, but he lathered up the best he could, scrubbing from balls to bald as his old man used to say.

By the time he stepped out of the shower he felt human again, even if his head still ached and it would be a while before he wanted to eat. He pictured that sleek torso, those mariner eyes. Maybe he'd get lucky after all.

He looked for his jeans, which he was pretty sure he would have left in a heap on the floor. They hung neatly across the back of a chair. He was shrugging on his tee when The Guy returned carrying coffees.

He handed one to Max and produced creamers and sugar packets from the pocket of his sweats. He held them out. "I didn't know how you like your coffee, or what passes for coffee here."

Max shook his head. "Thanks. Black's fine."

The Guy shrugged with an elegant lift of his shoulders. He placed his own coffee on the desk and began opening sugar packets. "It's all piss water anyway."

Max watched The Guy's long fingers tear another sugar packet and cleared his throat. "Look, I...um..."

Blue eyes shone from beneath incredibly long lashes. The man shook his head and focused again on his coffee. "You don't remember anything from last night?"

Max started to protest, but what did it matter? He had to meet Smitty and Bones soon, and weather permitting, the plane would finally leave for McMurdo early the next morning. The best he could hope for from this particular encounter would be a quick fuck, after which he'd never see The Guy again. Not that Max ever kept in touch anyway. Love-'em-and-leave-'em worked for lovers, for family, for the whole fucking waste of humanity.

Max shrugged. "Sorry. I must have had one too many last night."

The man chuckled. "Ten too many is more like it." He picked up his coffee and sipped, wrinkling his nose at the taste.

Max sipped his own coffee. It could have been stronger, but the acrid promise of caffeine was enough. He stepped closer.

His host looked at him for a long moment. "When I met you, you were entertaining the bar with wild stories. You told me your buddies had found women to entertain them and you were alone. You were too drunk to find your way home. I brought you here."

Relief washed through Max. Bones and Smitty must have been gone before this guy appeared. Max squinted at him, trying to remember. "You were just a good Samaritan?"

The Guy arched an eyebrow. "Apparently. You were very friendly in the taxi but passed out as soon as we got here."

Max closed his eyes and let a wave of shame roll through him. He opened them to see The Guy watching him. "Look, I'm sorry about that." Max touched the barbed wire tattoo. "Can I make it up to you?"

The Guy looked down at Max's hand on his arm. He seemed to consider for a moment. Then, with a shake of his head he jerked his arm away. "This was a bad idea last night and a worse one this morning. I'm sorry. I simply can't get involved with a drinker. Besides, I'm leaving Christchurch soon."

Max bit back a defensive reply about how it sounded like he'd been interested in a drinker the night before. And who said anything about getting involved? Instead of either of these, he muttered, "Suit yourself."

The Guy looked at the bedside clock. "I need to get ready."

Max swallowed the dregs, crumpled his cup, and tossed it toward the wastebasket. Without looking to see if he'd made the shot, he grabbed his scuffed leather jacket. "Yeah, me too. Thanks for the coffee and for giving me a place to sleep last night."

His host walked to the door and opened it. With a nod, Max left, wincing as it clicked shut behind him. He scowled at the closed door. Fucker had turned him down. Sanctimonious prick. He located the exit sign and marched off to find a taxi.

* * *

"How'd it go last night, Max?" Bones scooped a huge forkful of eggs into his mouth. "That redhead with the tits was eyeing you when we left."

Smitty laughed and wagged a sausage at Bones. "Come on, man. We scored the best pussy in the place. Don't rub the poor guy's nose in it."

Bones grinned back. "It looked like some fine stuff you were getting ready to rub your nose in when last I saw you."

Max closed his eyes and sent a grateful prayer to the angels who protect closeted divers. Eggs drenched in hot sauce, bacon, and a pot of baked beans, along with a gallon of strong coffee, were taking the edge off his hangover. He looked at his two companions. Max had nicknamed Dave Bonair "Bones" the first summer they'd worked together. The name— an ironic comment on the huge man's bulk—had stuck. A person would need to chisel through a lot of muscle and a layer of fat to get to his bones. On the other hand, Smitty— whose mother had actually saddled him with the innocuous name of John Smith—was built from bone and lean muscle, a wiry rat of a man whose face showed all forty-seven of his wind-beaten years.

Max shook his head. He slathered his toast with jam. "A gentleman never reveals a lady's indiscretions."

Bones grinned at him. "You old horndog. I knew it."

Smitty shrugged. "Gotta get it while we can, right? No telling what the pickins will be like once we're on station." He winked at Max. "Although I bet Annie's anxious to get some diver dick after a dark, cold winter."

Max nodded and bit into his toast. It was going to be another long summer.

Chapter Two

Max watched the night through the window as the bus ferried them from the support team headquarters, where he'd filled a locker with the clothing and gear he wouldn't need in Antarctica, to IAC—the International Antarctic Center—a distance of less than a mile that always felt longer because it meant leaving civilization and the warm spring air of New Zealand behind for the institutionalized freezer that was Antarctica. For Max, it also meant putting his libido on hold and burrowing deep into the closet for the six months the dive team would be on station at McMurdo. But it was worth the price, because underneath that icy continent lay his beautiful deep blue playground.

At four in the morning, the IAC looked like any other flight terminal until you got inside and found yourself shuffling down a corridor to be outfitted with thirty-five pounds of fashionable orange and black cold-weather gear. Max and the rest of the crew were part of the winter fly-in—WinFly—the first flight to the continent in six months. Most of them were destined for a season on Ross Island at McMurdo Station, while a handful would travel on to the South Pole. Their job would be to prepare the stations for the main season, when scientists would arrive for a few hectic months of research studying the ways the changing climate was shrinking the whole goddamned continent. Right now, the skeletal crews overwintering at McMurdo and the South Pole station were no doubt looking forward to an influx of fresh produce and an opportunity to restock the liquor cabinets.

About a hundred people milled around the waiting area, chatting and laughing, stuffing extra clothing into their duffels or slumping sleepily in molded plastic chairs. Bones and Smitty sauntered off to try their charms on a clutch of young women. Max dropped his bag and leaned against the wall.

A thrum of excitement bounced around the room. First-timers chattered like nervous crows, their eagerness high-pitched and volatile. Returning snowbirds like Max stood alone or in quiet groups emitting bass notes of joy. They were going home.

The plane wouldn't leave for a few more hours. Max was used to waiting. A decade in the military had accustomed him to hurry up and wait. Of course, most of that time he'd been a SEAL, and the hurry-up had been adrenaline-fueled and often bloody. The blood. That was what still haunted him most.

He gazed around the room. There was the usual weird jumble of hippies, jocks, and geeks who'd found their way to the bottom of the world. Max recognized a couple of people from past years, but he was in no hurry to greet them. There'd be time later. Life in Antarctica was all about togetherness.

As Max was wondering where they got cold-weather gear to fit the tall, skinny guy, he turned, and Max recognized the wild mop of hair and long, thin nose. Max's stomach fell. He swore under his breath. The Guy shifted, and when his gaze hit on Max, he paled, his lip curled, and he looked away. At least the feeling was mutual. Maybe they could avoid each other. At McMurdo. For months. Christ.

Eventually the call came, and they all shuffled out to the *swish* of a couple hundred nylon-clad thighs rubbing together. As many boots clomped across the tarmac, like a line of black-and-orange bugs crawling into the round belly of the Herc—the squat military transport plane that ferried cooks, janitors, computer jockeys, scientists, and divers to the frozen continent, Max climbed the short steps into the beast and snagged a seat against the wall near the front, which gave him a clear view of the door. Almost eight years since he left the SEALs, but the training was drilled into his bones. Always know what's behind you and what's coming next. He strapped himself in and leaned into the elastic webbing that stretched the length of the plane and served as their only seat back.

Max watched the man who could ruin his life duck his head as he passed through the door, look around the plane, and shuffle toward a seat in the back. As usual, despite the fact this was the only flight until October, the plane wasn't anywhere near capacity. Bones and Smitty had scored spots with supply boxes strapped into the seats on either side, and Max watched them settling in for the five-hour flight, thankfully a long way from The Guy. At least the three of them wouldn't be chatting on the way down. Homophobia was a trait ingrained in every diver Max had ever known. He needed to have a word with The Guy before he interacted with Max's redneck colleagues.

It was only when the hatch closed and the plane engines roared to life that Max relaxed. He took a long pull from his hip flask and slipped in a pair of earplugs. The woman next to him pulled out an e-book reader. Max took one more glance around the plane, decided he was safe for the moment, closed his eyes, and imagined the clear blue water of the Antarctic Ocean.

The early morning flight was timed to get them to the sea ice runway at noon, during the brief gray daylight. Max woke, feeling a subtle shift in the vibration of the engines. People around him stirred. Even without windows to look out, he knew they were descending, could feel the altitude drop in his belly. His ears popped. He braced his legs in preparation for landing and saw the other experienced Antarcticans doing the same. The plane leveled, dropped, leveled, dropped, and hit with a *thud*. Someone laughed. The woman beside him gasped and clutched her elbow, which must have poked through the orange netting holding them all in place, to bang against the plane wall. Max's teeth clattered as the plane bounced along the icy runway. For a military landing, it wasn't bad, but the civilians didn't look too happy about the bumps.

The plane slowed and stopped. The engines cut. Max removed his earplugs. The pilot announced the local temperature was -30 Fahrenheit, winds only 10 mph. Max shrugged back into his jacket as the door opened onto a balmy August day in Antarctica.

He pulled a balaclava over his mouth and nose, tightened his jacket hood so that only his eyes were exposed, and slipped on his goggles. Around him, his fellow passengers were doing the same. The rustle of clothing sounded loud in the quiet cabin. Max unstrapped himself from the wall, hooked an arm through his duffel, took a deep breath, and launched himself up and out into the cold. He inhaled the frigid air and felt his heart swell as he surveyed the flat white valley rimmed by jagged peaks. God, it was good to be back.

He loped down the steps, and his boots crunched on the snowy runway. His clothing flapped in the wind. The lights of McMurdo Station twinkled in the distance through the gray twilight that defined daytime this time of year. A giant yellow forklift edged up to the rear of the plane. The whine and clang of the tail door opening echoed through the air, followed by metal tongs clanking against the deck as they slipped under the first crate of supplies.

Max took his place beside Bones in an assembly line of passengers passing out the extra bags of foodstuffs and supplies that had been strapped into every available seat. They loaded the supplies into the back of a large red van with huge rubber wheels that always made McMurdo Station vehicles look like the toy trucks Max's brother had thwacked him on the head with back in the day. As they finished, the enormous Terra Bus rumbled to a stop. The door opened, and a small figure bundled in red, black and yellow sprang out.

Bones jabbed Max in the ribs, a move made fairly ineffective by their layers of insulation. "See? Told ya she'd be jonesing for you."

Max rolled his eyes, but he smiled as he stepped forward and swung Annie Shea up into a hug. When he put her down, she nodded toward his fellow travelers, who were filing past them and onto the big red van. "Can't say I'm glad to have all these people invading. But it's nice to see you, Mac." She'd given him the nickname the first time she saw the initials he'd marked in black ink on his duffel: M.A.C. It wasn't a name he allowed from anyone else.

"Nice to see you too." And he meant it. Annie and that cold blue ocean -- that was what kept bringing him back to McMurdo. His best friend and his favorite dream. He eyed the line. The Guy was talking with a few of the other newbies. Maybe they'd bond and Max wouldn't have to worry about him for a while.

"Well, don't stand around here freezing. Let's go." Annie waved him into the line of people shuffling forward.

When everyone was in, Annie swung up into the bus, closing the door behind her. She faced the group and flipped off her hood. Someone inhaled sharply, the noise level dropped, and Max wondered again what it would feel like to have people react that strongly to the sight of you. After all this time, he barely noticed the scar that puckered the skin and twisted her lip up and eye down, but he doubted Annie ever forgot.

She looked at them without expression, slid into the driver's seat, and with a grind and a lurch, they were off. Annie's voice, devoid of inflection, sounded over the van speakers. "Welcome to McMurdo. If you've been here before, you know the drill. For those of you sampling the bottom of the world for the first time, lunch now, after which you'll be briefed on how we live down here and get a room assignment. Sunset starts in a couple hours. Should be pretty. You might want to check it out."

The heat from their bodies and moisture from their breath crystallized ice on the windows. Through the windshield, Max watched the black crud of McMurdo appear. Lights shone from the cluster of mismatched buildings, lending an unexpected warmth to the general mining-town ambience of the place. Day had come back to Antarctica, and in a few months it would completely replace the night. Excited chatter swelled around him as Antarctic veterans pointed out sights to wide-eyed newcomers.

The Terra Bus ground to a halt. Max waited while everyone disembarked. He watched Bones and Smitty sprint toward building 155, undoubtedly hoping to avoid standing in line for food. The Guy strolled more slowly, apparently engrossed in conversation with a middle-aged man Max recognized as having worked computer support the year before.

The last puffy jacket descended the bus steps, and Max stood. He walked up the aisle to join Annie. "How was your winter?"

"Nice. Quiet. Dark. Can't say I'm looking forward to all the bright lights and people." She cocked an eyebrow at him. "Did you bring me anything?"

He smiled. "It's in my bag."

The side of her face that moved broke into a wide grin. She patted his arm. "That's my boy. Now let's go in before your scummy friends eat everything."

After lunch, the air would fill with the churn of engines, the clank of metal, and the slosh of tires through the volcanic mud, but while everyone ate, the station was quiet. Max and Annie crossed the lot to building 155. Inside, Max inhaled deeply. It smelled of institutional carpet, the wet-dog odor of drying parkas, and ancient cooking smells, a mixture so familiar that he instantly felt at home.

He took in the college dorm-style decor. On a corkboard by the recreational office, colorful posters advertised activities from ceramics to band practice. There was a sign-up sheet recruiting volunteers for the library and flyers notifying the community of the availability of various part-time jobs.

The hallway stretched before him. He could hear the clatter of conversation in the dining room. "What's for lunch?"

Annie snorted. "Hamburgers, veggie burgers, and chili. Same thing we've had for the last week and a half. I hope that plane of yours brought some fruit, eggs, and milk that haven't been dehydrated yet. I'm tired of chili for lunch and oatmeal for breakfast."

"I'm sure it did. The bacon hold out this year?" He waved to a woman he recognized from last year who looked up from a computer terminal. She smiled briefly and returned to her screen. It would be a while before the winter-overs, used to the intimate company of each other, were comfortable with the newcomers. One planeload doubled the station population. Max knew from past experience that there'd be grumbling about lines for food and crowding in the dorms until the new crowd was absorbed into the old. And it would all happen again in another couple of months when the bulk of the researchers arrived, swelling the population from three- to four-digit numbers.

Annie hung her coat on a hook in one of the outerwear alcoves. He hung his beside hers. "This year it was steak. The meal plans got mixed up, and we had steak nearly every night for most of June and not once since then. Dinner tonight is supposed to be beef stroganoff, but I'm betting that's scrapped for steak, sautéed veggies, and fresh fruit. I'm sick of hydroponic cucumbers and tomatoes. I can taste the oranges now."

They climbed the steps to the cafeteria and took their places at the end of the line, which was moving quickly. Max's stomach grumbled, and he realized it had been a long time since he'd eaten. Even McMurdo hamburgers and chili sounded good.

Annie laughed at the giant bowl with which Max approached the Frosty Boy. He grinned at her. "Come on, it's been a long time."

She shook her head. "And do you go out of your way to find soft-serve ice cream up north?"

He shrugged. "Not since I was a kid. But this is Frosty Boy. It's like an icon or something."

She gestured toward the dining room. "Okay, Mr. Icon. Where do you want to sit? If it's with the troglodytes, you can count me out. How you stand those Neanderthals is beyond me."

Max considered. There were several empty tables, and he knew Annie wouldn't mind sitting alone, would probably prefer it, but he thought it sent the wrong signal for the first day. Bones and Smitty's table was full. Even if Annie had wanted to, that wasn't an option.

"What is this, high school?" Annie shook her head and headed right for the only table Max did not want to sit at, the one with two open chairs, a middle-aged computer geek Max knew from the year before, a young man he hadn't met, and The Guy.

They passed a table of people Max recognized as part of the winter staff. One of the men whistled and called out good-naturedly, "Well, look who's back. Little Annie's gonna be a happy girl tonight."

"Shut up, you moron." She swiped at him with her napkin.

Max glanced at The Guy, who was watching him, his mouth puckered as if he found his lunch revolting. Annie slid into her seat, and Max found himself sitting across from The Guy.

It was always instructive to watch new people with Annie. Most people looked away or held their faces rigid and smiled unconvincingly. That was certainly the case for the kid, Henrick Krause, a big blond whose eyes skittered across her face as he mumbled hello.

The Guy, who introduced himself as Andre Dubois, greeted her with genuine warmth. His gaze didn't turn cold until it found Max.

"We've met." His tone chilled Max more than his Frosty Boy. "Although I expect Mr. Conway would not remember."

The table seemed to wait for more, but neither of them said anything, and the conversation moved on. Max's head started to hurt.

Annie turned to Andre. "Where are you from?"

Andre's eyes warmed again as he turned to her. "That's a complicated question for me to answer. I was born and grew up in Paris, my father moved us to Switzerland when I was in secondary school, I went to university in the States, completed a postdoc at the Max Planck Institute in Bremen, and now I'm at UC Davis in California."

She nodded. "We get a lot of that. It's the travelers that fall off the globe and end up here."

Andre smiled at her. "Where do you come from?"

"Nowhere special. The States." Annie's face closed up.

He leaned back, as if allowing her some distance, and turned toward Henrick. "It's the same with you, eh? Only one nationality?"

Henrick's smile was haughty even as he licked a dollop of mustard from his thumb. "As your President Kennedy said, '*Ich bin ein Berliner.*'"

Annie's chair scraped against the linoleum as she stood. "There's a difference between us, Henrick. I don't belong anywhere but here."

* * *

The briefing was dull but blessedly short, and afterward Max joined Annie in their shared room. Theirs was a complicated friendship, built on mutual need and traded favors. It had started Max's first year when he stepped in to protect Annie from a drunken and particularly obnoxious suitor and had developed into the perfect cover for both of them. He'd moved in as Annie's roommate his second year on the ice. Max kept the sharks from Annie's door, and she furnished his closet. When anyone asked why they'd never pushed their twin beds together, Annie explained that Max snored. And Max periodically picked up condoms at the dispensary, which he tucked into his luggage and took off the ice for use in the bars back home.

The room was a burst of color after the beige sameness of the dorm hallway. Annie had crammed the small room with the sparkly trinkets people brought her from the world above. As far as Max knew, she hadn't left Antarctica in years. It was against the rules to keep someone down here year after year with no breaks, but the rules never quite applied to Annie.

"So?" she asked, as Max swung his duffel onto his bed.

He smiled and dug through his luggage until he located the card. He handed it to her. She opened the generic birthday card, laughed at the predictable joke, and peeled off the false backing. Her eyes gleamed as she brought it out.

"It took me a while to find. He's moved." He gestured toward the white blotter paper that contained a dozen hits of the best LSD available. He didn't mention the sweat that broke out in the small of his back every time he passed through customs with enough contraband to send him away for a very long time.

"Then these are special." She held the page up to the light reverently, as if greeting each individual impregnated dot. She placed the sheet in her carved sandalwood East Indian box and tucked it deep into her underwear drawer. She smiled at him. "Thank you. You know how much this means to me."

"I also brought you this." He held out a bright yellow mermaid made from papier-mâché and a coconut shell.

She held out her hand. "You went to Mexico?"

He shook his head. "I did some salvage work out of San Diego. That's as far south as I got."

She leaned up on her tiptoes and kissed his cheek. "Thank you. Your present's under the bed. They ran out of everything but gin last month."

Alcohol was about the only thing you could spend money on at McMurdo, and like everywhere else, it was cheaper by the bottle. McMurdo rules limited residents to one bottle of booze per week. After that, the only way you could get it was in one of the two bars, by the glass. Other than periodic acid trips, which she claimed were her spiritual release, Annie was as sober as they came. Max wasn't. And a bottle a week didn't do it. All winter Annie dutifully bought her weekly bottle, sometimes scotch, more often rum or gin—

it depended on what was available at the time—and tucked it under his bed.

Rationing. It helped Max stay in control. With the bottles under the bed, her weekly bottle and his own, Max kept his drinking down to three fifths a week plus the occasional night out. He even shared his booze with Bones and Smitty sometimes. Just like they shared theirs with him. Stateside it didn't matter how much he drank. Every now and then he'd show up drunk and get canned from some piss-ass job cleaning piers or inspecting bridges. But it didn't matter. He could always find another crap dive job. There wasn't another Antactica. Like balancing on a teeter-totter—six months living the life of a relatively sober monk, the other six doing whatever the fuck he wanted. Half the year in the deep blue water, the rest in a murky cesspool. It was all about the trade-off.

Max pulled out the rubber bin and began examining the bottles one by one. He held up a fifth of lovely amber liquid with a distinctive gold label. "This must have cost you a pretty penny."

She shrugged. "I thought you'd like it. I got them while they lasted. I think it was about three weeks. There's some nice bourbon in there that I thought would match your eyes."

When he first applied to work at McMurdo, Max had been shocked at the low salaries. He'd expected serious hazard pay for working at such an isolated field site. Still, free room and board and nothing but booze to spend a paycheck on meant most people went home with a stash. Annie, of course, never went home. If she ever did, she'd be loaded.

Max replaced the tequila and pulled out a bottle of bourbon. "I'll save that for a special occasion. But this will do nicely tonight." He held it next to his face for her to see. "What do you think?"

Annie laughed. "Perfect. Except the bourbon isn't bloodshot."

"It hasn't just flown in from New Zealand." He twisted the cap, breaking the seal with a snap. He sniffed. It smelled rich and clean, like leather armchairs in old-fashioned smoking rooms. Max upended the bottle and took a long, appreciative swig.

"You are such a bum." Annie laughed, flopping back onto her bed. "Tell me about the tall, very sexy, probably gay science type you've already pissed off. What did you do, step on his toes getting on the plane?"

Max set the bottle on his bedside table and started unpacking his duffel. He exaggerated the man's accent. "Andre?"

"Oh, Christ. Don't tell me you slept with him."

Max spun and stared at her. It wasn't a good idea to forget that Annie read people like others read books. She wasn't psychic. She'd earned her powers of observation during the kind of childhood you only survived if you were very good at knowing what was going on. She knew people instantly. And for the most part, she didn't like them.

Max opened his mouth to explain.

A fist pounded against the door, startling them both. Smitty's reedy voice echoed in from the hallway. "Take a break, lovebirds. The chief wants to see us stat."

Annie shrugged. She tousled her hair, undid the top button of her shirt, and leaned against the bed in a very good imitation of a ravished woman interrupted. She winked at him.

Max grinned, untucked his shirt, and opened the door. Tucking his shirt back into his jeans, he growled, "All right, all right, I heard you."

Bones craned his head over Smitty's shoulder. Max let them get one peak at Annie as he grabbed his coat. He muscled them out and closed the door behind him.

Bones gave him a punch in the shoulder and grinned. This was the second season for Bones and third for Smitty. In the beginning of their tenure on the ice, each had made a single derogatory statement about Annie's face and paid for it with pain. Bones had been schooled as a commercial diver and Smitty as a recreational dive instructor. They were tough, brave, and strong in their own ways. But Max was a fucking Navy SEAL. All right, an ex-SEAL, but still not a man to cross, particularly when he'd had a few. They knew now that when it came to Annie, they should be respectful.

* * *

The chief, Frank Jackson, was a Navy diver who'd set depth records in his day. Sixty, grizzled, and five feet four on a good morning, he had balls the size of Texas. The first time

Max met him, Jackson had declared his disdain for the SEALs. "Bunch of testosterone junkies" was the term he used.

When Max had agreed that "Yes, sir, that about covered it," Jackson had narrowed his eyes. "Smart-ass, are you?"

"Not smart at all, sir." Max had kept Jackson's gaze. "If I'd had any brains, I wouldn't have worked hard to become lead diver only to end my career in a desert war."

Jackson had guffawed at that and set about making Max prove himself in a grueling series of under-ice dives. They tested every piece of equipment on Ross Island, sometimes staying below until Max had sucked down all but the last few breaths of air. Invariably he'd have to swallow his pride and show Chief Jackson his depleted gauge. And, as invariably, the old man could have stayed down much longer. In the end, Max had to admit the chief was a better diver and a damned tough old man.

When Bones and Smitty came along, Jackson hadn't put either of them through his personal version of BUD/S— the six months of hell every sailor had to pass through if he wanted to be a SEAL. He wasn't gentle on them exactly. Most of the time, he left them alone. Max might be a damned arrogant SEAL, but at least he was Navy.

Jackson looked up as the three entered his tiny, sterile office. "Afternoon."

Like they'd seen each other the day before, not six full months earlier.

Max took the chair across from Chief Jackson, leaving Bones and Smitty to lean against the wall. "Afternoon, sir. How was your winter?"

Chief Jackson shrugged. "Dark." He shuffled through the stack of papers on his desk. "The new safety officer won't arrive until October. For now, we're in charge of orientation. About half the folks who came in on your plane are snowbirds like you. I'll be doing the refresher course for them tonight. The rest are virgins, which means we need to put them through their paces. There are thirty of them. I'll take half." He glanced up. "Mr. Smith, you can help me." He pulled a sheet of paper from the stack and passed it to Max. "You and Bonair will take the others. We'll all meet at 0800 tomorrow for the lecture. After that we'll split up and take the groups to the ice shelf for Happy Camper School. Any questions?"

"No, sir." Max read through the names on his sheet. Just his luck, Andre fucking Dubois.

Chief Jackson waved a finger at Max's list. "For the bulk of them, this is the closest they'll get to the great ice adventure. This first wave is mostly janitors, desk jockeys, and mechanics. But we've got an eager-beaver scientist and his student that I want you to pay special attention to. God knows why they couldn't wait for mainbody like everyone else, but there you go. Guy's name's Dubois, and his student is something German like Krauss. As I understand it, they want to set up a field site at the edge of the ice shelf. Try and make sure they know enough to survive out there."

Max stared at him. "What do you mean, they're setting up a field station? There won't be enough daylight to do that for another month."

"Be that as it may."

Max shook his head. "But that's crazy."

Chief Jackson's smile was grim. "I can't say I disagree with you, son. But we're here to support them, not the other way around."

Max grimaced and stood. "We'll get the equipment ready for tomorrow."

Chief Jackson turned his attention back to the pile of paperwork on his desk. "You do that. Take a generator and set up lights around the Happy Camper warming hut. Gonna be dark out there tomorrow. The sooner we get this over with, the sooner we can start checking the dive equipment. There's a long season ahead."

Max nodded. He wasn't looking forward to either Happy Camper or the equipment checks. But they both needed to happen before he could slip back into those dark blue waters.

Chapter Three

Running Happy Camper—the two-day survival training required of everyone at McMurdo—was a piece of cake on long summer days in December when the sun never set, but much more of a challenge in August, when Mount Erebus obscured what little sun appeared and life on Ross Island never brightened beyond twilight.

Chief Jackson spent the morning lecturing the group on ice survival basics. Max found himself glancing far too often at Andre. With his long, thin nose, he looked severe in profile, but Max had seen the lean lines of his body, and it was an image he couldn't get out of his mind.

Max pounded down the foggy feeling in his head with yet another cup of coffee. He, Smitty, and Bones had killed the bourbon over a few rounds in the tiny, warped bowling alley. It wasn't enough to get seriously drunk, but he'd gotten a nice buzz, and this morning his head was taking a while to clear, a fact Dr. Great Body/Small Mind Dubois didn't need to know.

At a signal from Chief Jackson, Max and Smitty set out to get the vans. Max zipped up his bright orange survival suit.

The temperature outside hovered in the negative twenties, warm for this time of the year. With Smitty trailing behind, he stepped out into the predawn gray. The hum of a generator filled the air. Someone started an engine. It would be over an hour before the sun rose behind Mount Erebus and lightened the sky. They'd better get moving if they wanted to take advantage of the light.

The Happy Campers chatted nervously as they trudged into the vans. Probably scared of spending the night outside at forty below. Bones had collared Henrick and another strapping young man to help distribute box lunches for the drive out to the ice shelf. With less than three hours of available daylight, they couldn't afford to squander even a minute of field time on food.

The outline of the horizon was barely visible as they pulled the vehicles up to the warming hut. Chief Jackson and Smitty took their crew north. Max led his troop to the southern site. Bones loped off to get the snowmobile and pull a sled heaped with tents, sleeping bags, and supplies to the campsite. It was cold and still. The snow crunched loudly beneath their feet. Max's own breath echoed inside his hood.

He stopped and turned, gesturing for the others to circle around. Fifteen nearly identical puffy orange figures with black-masked faces stared at him. He pointed toward a series of wavy ice ridges barely visible in the distance. "There are huge crevasses over there. Many of them are covered by thin layers of ice and snow. Last year a man fell in, about fifty feet. A blizzard blew up, and it was thirty-six hours before we could get to him. He broke his leg and got sent home on the next flight, but he survived because he'd paid attention during Happy Camper training. Stay within the area defined by the flagged poles." He waved toward the yellow flag one hundred yards away. "That's the restroom. We cart everything back to the station. Please use the poop barrel and pee bucket. You might want to grab a pee jar for inside your tent or trench. You wouldn't want to get lost heading for the john if a snowstorm blows up in the middle of the night."

He broke them into teams to set up tents and start building snow trenches. If this was like any other group, most people would opt to sleep in the tents, but the few who built themselves trenches—grave-like caves in the snow—would have a warmer night. He paired Andre with a small woman who had identified herself as a cook and Henrick with the janitor who'd helped him load box lunches, deciding it would be better to separate them. They both needed strong survival skills.

Henrick and the janitor worked with two other men on the Scott tent—an old-fashioned pyramid of the type used by the first Antarctic explorers. Silly to choose sentiment over practicality, but he didn't tell them that. It was their discomfort. The subzero sleeping bags they all had would keep everyone from freezing to death, but those drafty old tents wouldn't help much.

Andre, on the other hand, had apparently talked his companion into a trench and was sawing big blocks out of the snow. Out here on the ice shelf, wind packed the snow so firmly that you could cut perfect squares that looked like giant Styrofoam building blocks. By digging down and building up, it was possible to make a cozy sleeping cave out of the wind and be at least somewhat protected from the cold.

The crews chatted and laughed while they worked. The light grew. Almost immediately it dimmed, and the sky turned a brilliant fiesta orange. Andre stopped shoveling and stood still, staring up at the sky.

Max stepped close to him. "Nice, eh?"

Andre jumped. The shoveling must have warmed him because he'd taken off his balaclava. In the reflected light of the sunset, his eyes looked dark, not the brilliant blue they appeared in daylight.

"Wow," the woman beside Andre gushed. "That's amazing."

Andre turned to her. Max could see the edge of his smile. "I've read about these nacreous clouds. They're formed from nitric acid and water. The nitric acid crystallizes in the atmosphere. It results in refraction of the light."

Max rolled his eyes. Know-it-all scientists. "It also means it's going to be a cold-ass night. You'd better get back to work."

"Thank you for your advice." Andre glanced back at the trailer where the staff stayed. "I take it you'll be spending your evening in the warming hut?"

He made it sound like Max was a goddamned wimp. Max straightened. "I've done my time and slept in more extreme environments than you'll ever know."

"That must be challenging for you." Andre raised an eyebrow. "I would imagine drinking is dangerous out here."

"Fuck you." It came out before he could stop himself.

The cook looked from one to the other. "You guys know each other?"

"No," Max said firmly as Andre answered, "We've met."

Max stomped away, his heart pounding. Andre constituted a serious threat. Max imagined everything he'd built over the years crumbling in an instant. If he wanted to keep coming back to this continent he loved, he had to get the asshole alone and make him promise to keep his damned mouth shut. And enough about the drinking. Christ, the guy had a real obsession. Max had to convince him to keep it zipped. Of course, getting alone time with someone wasn't exactly an easy thing to do in Antarctica. On this huge fucking continent the people were packed together tightly enough that finding somewhere to jack off was a major endeavor and having sex required as much planning as a hundred foot dive. He paused. *Okay, where did that thought come from? He wasn't having sex in Antarctica. Not with anyone, especially not some high-and-mighty scientist who thought he drank too much.*

Max shook his head and moved to the next cluster of people. He needed to get their tents checked before he could set up for the stove-lighting demonstration. And he could use a drink. Except drinking during Happy Camper School was not only against every rule, out here on the shelf, Andre was right, it was downright dangerous. Max took survival seriously. All he brought out onto the ice was a shot a day, just enough to keep away the heebie-jeebies. And he'd have to wait for that until just before bed, when the chief was out of the trailer making his final rounds.

The sunset lingered for a few hours and disappeared by the time everyone had figured out how to melt snow for tea and cook their freeze-dried dinner. Max fired up the gasoline generator that powered a halogen lamp. Chief Jackson's camp shone as a beacon to the north, and the lights of McMurdo glistened in the distance. The generator hummed. Darkness loomed thick outside the blue-white pool of illumination. Clusters of campers returned to work, finishing their frosty accommodations.

Max spotted Andre heading up the trail to the yellow flag. He followed, his footfalls loud in his own ears. He stopped twenty feet from the pole and waited. The wind picked up, blowing snow into his eyes as he squinted up the trail. Andre turned and started back. He stopped when he saw Max.

"I need to talk to you," Max said quickly, unsure whether Andre recognized him in the generic orange and black suit.

Andre inclined his head but said nothing.

Max cleared his throat. "Look. I know we didn't get off on the right foot and all, but I need you to keep that whole night a secret."

Andre crossed his arms over his chest. "You don't want people to know you passed out drunk?"

"No, not that. It's where I was when it happened that I'd rather no one knew." He paused. Andre waited. "Tell people I passed out if you like. But not in your bed."

Andre gave a sharp laugh. "Do you think that I want to brag about taking you home? It was a momentary lapse in judgment."

Max grimaced at the insult.

Andre continued, "I understand the drinking; we all have our defects of character. But I don't know how you could do that to your charming girlfriend. I think she's had enough pain in her life."

Max shook his head. "It's not like that. We're not…it's complicated. But no one here knows I'm gay."

Andre stared at him, the light from camp reflecting in his eyes. "In other words, you're not a cheat, but you are a coward. I suppose I should be happy for her."

Max's anger rose hot and fast. He'd been called a lot of things in his day, but a coward? His muscles tightened. If he hit the guy, he'd probably be fired on the spot and sent north. It wasn't worth it. He consciously unclenched his fists.

"Don't worry. I won't tell anyone about your secret." Andre brushed past him. "How you live your life is none of my business. As long as you keep it away from me. I can't afford to get tangled up in your drama."

Max watched him for a long time, a dark solitary figure moving toward the light.

* * *

Wind rattling the windows of the warming hut woke Max. He lay listening to it blowing past. Turning onto his side, he saw Chief Jackson sit up in the next cot.

"Hope they're huddled together over in the Scott tent." The old man peered at his watch. "Let's give it another hour before we wake them up. Maybe in the meantime the damn wind will calm down."

Max sat up. "I'll make coffee."

"Quietly. I'd like a little morning peace before the children wake." Chief Jackson gestured toward the other two cots. Smitty lay on his back issuing dainty snorts, and Bones was buried deep in the down.

Max smiled. At forty-seven and twenty-eight respectively, Smitty and Bones weren't exactly children. For that matter, Smitty was a hell of a lot older than Max. And if that was how Chief Jackson thought of them, did that mean he considered Max a grown-up? At thirty-four, he should be. But whether or not he acted like an adult depended on who you asked.

Despite the cold morning and cramped sleeping arrangements, he felt great. He should try going to bed sober more often. Or almost sober. A single shot wasn't enough to count. He turned his back to Chief Jackson as he pulled his dick through the openings in his layers of long underwear and filled his pee jar. He hoisted himself off the bed and into the black overalls of his survival suit. It wasn't exactly warm in the hut, but at least the water they'd hauled from the station hadn't frozen overnight.

The Happy Campers could brew their own coffee by boiling snow on tiny survival stoves, but it seemed cruel to make them wait for something hot to drink after a long, cold night in the tents. And besides, the hut had one of those church basement thirty-cup coffeemakers left by some kindhearted soul many Happy Camper Schools ago. Max filled it with water and coffee and plugged it in.

As the scent of fresh coffee filled the hut, Smitty sat and stretched. Beside him, Bones rustled in his sleeping bag.

"What time is it?" Bones asked, his voice muffled and his nose poking over the edge of his sleeping bag.

Chief Jackson sat on the edge of his cot, cramming his bag into a stuff sack. "Ah, it's Tweedledee and Tweedledumb, up at the crack of"—he consulted his watch—"0723. It's the early bird that catches the worm."

Smitty made a face at Chief Jackson's back and wriggled out of his bag.

Bones laughed. "I'd like some bird to catch my worm, all right."

"I gotta take a dump." Smitty started pulling on his survival suit.

Chief Jackson gestured toward the outside. "I suggest you hold it, Mr. Smith. This wind is scheduled to die down around 0800. Right now I'm guessing you'd have a hard time finding your way."

Smitty groaned and flopped back on his cot. "I'm going back to sleep."

* * *

Max was on his second cup of coffee when the wind suddenly ceased rattling the hut walls. He was about to suggest they wake Smitty when a sharp banging erupted against the metal door. Max had his hand on the knob when the door flew open, and there stood the janitor from the Scott tent, his face red from the cold.

"Henrick's gone," he blurted through chattering teeth. "We can't find him anywhere."

Max hauled the man into the hut and closed the door. He shoved his own coffee cup into his hands. "Drink this. You need to warm up."

The man nodded and took a long sip.

Chief Jackson put a hand on his arm. "Now what's this about Henrick?"

The janitor's hands shook as he cupped them around Max's mug. "None of us slept very well last night. It was friggin' cold. Henrick got up about an hour ago, said he was gonna burst if he didn't go pee." He bit his lip.

"Go on." The chief's voice was soft. "It's Roger, right?"

Roger nodded. "I must have fallen back asleep. When I woke, Henrick wasn't back. The wind wasn't as strong. I figured I'd find him when I went to the yellow pole myself." His eyes widened as he continued. "Only he wasn't there. He wasn't anywhere. The other guys in the Scott tent and I, we looked everywhere."

Chief Jackson caught Max's eye, and the message was clear. They'd better find him quick.

"I'll start the generator, get some light on the camp." Max shrugged on his coat.

Jackson nodded. He turned to Bones and gestured at Smitty. "Get him up. You two can hand out flashlights and get everyone buddied up. No one leaves camp without a buddy, got it?"

Roger started to move, but Chief Jackson pushed him toward a cot. "You stay here. I don't need any more cases of hypothermia than absolutely necessary. Are your friends from the tent still out looking?"

At Roger's nod, Max said, "I'll round them up and get them back here as quickly as possible, sir."

The chief shook his head. "I'll take care of them. You get south camp up and searching. They're your people."

"Yes, sir." Max flew out the door and trotted toward the generator. It took a few pulls to get the frozen mechanism firing, but soon cool halogen light bathed the camp. Blown by the wind, snow piled against the eastern side of the tents. Heads emerged from tent flaps. Figures appeared dressed in black pants and orange coats. Smitty arrived with a bin of flashlights, and Max began pairing up the searchers.

Snow puffed from the entrance to a trench, and Andre climbed out.

Max grabbed two flashlights from Smitty. "You stay here and hand out these. Get people looking to the north. Keep them away from the ridges. That's where I'm headed in case he fell in."

The wind blew swirls of snow around their feet, the noise strong enough to muffle conversation. Max closed the distance between himself and Andre.

"Your student's missing." A sudden lull in the wind made the words sound harsher than he'd intended.

Andre's brows furrowed. "Missing?"

Max thrust a flashlight into Andre's hand. "He got lost on his way to the pole. He's your student and my responsibility. There's only one area where he could get seriously hurt. You and I are looking there."

Andre nodded. "Of course." He switched on his light.

Max strode toward the ridges, not bothering to see whether Andre followed or not. Within moments, Andre was matching him step for step, swinging light in a slow arc before him. They walked in silence for a few minutes, the sound of the generator fading behind them, usurped by the crunch of their feet on the snow and the whip of their clothing in the wind.

Andre put a hand on Max's arm to stop him. He turned back toward the camp and considered for a long moment. "If he left his tent, heading toward the pole, and veered in this direction, he would not be down this far. We should look there." He pointed thirty degrees to the west.

Max looked back at the camp. The Scott tent was clearly visible in the pool of halogen light. He grunted. "People get turned around in the snow. There's no telling where he might be. Still, it's a place to start."

They turned and walked in the direction Andre had pointed. Max's breath sounded loud inside his hood. Hiking through snow always felt slow and hard. He listened to the swish of their clothing and squeak of boots in the snow.

"How did you end up with a German graduate student?" Max spoke into the relative silence.

Andre shrugged. "He was recommended by my postdoctoral adviser."

"Is he smart?" Max swept the landscape with his light. Nothing but snow and wind.

Andre hesitated slightly. "He wouldn't be here otherwise. His test scores are astronomical and his grades perfect."

"But?" Max glanced at Andre's sharp profile.

Andre shrugged. "Not everything can be learned in a book. There are times he seems somewhat...I don't know... overconfident?"

"You're not surprised he's in trouble?"

Andre was silent.

Max sighed. "Well, let's hope he remembered everything he learned yesterday."

"Yes."

Max's light fell on a ridge of snow, and he held out his hand to stop Andre. "Step carefully. We're near the crevasse zone."

Andre stilled. He'd clearly been paying attention the day before when Max had described the areas where thin sheets of ice disguised chasms in the snowpack.

"Henrick." The wind swallowed the sound of Andre's voice.

"Let's try it together." Max held up his gloved fingers. "On three."

They called, then listened. Nothing. Max picked his way forward, testing the ground with each step. Andre fell in beside him. Another ten yards and they called again, listened again.

Max felt the crack as Andre's foot broke through. Max threw an arm around him and flung them both to the ground. Andre exhaled with a whoosh as he hit the snow.

"You okay?" Max propped himself on one elbow and looked at Andre, his arm resting across Andre's chest. Even through all those layers of clothing, Andre felt solid and warm.

Andre didn't move away. He seemed to be catching his breath. "That's a terrible feeling, when your foot keeps going. Thank you."

Both men started as a foghorn split the air.

Max watched Andre's breath puff into the space between them. "They found your boy."

Andre closed his eyes and exhaled loudly. He opened them and looked at Max with a light smile. "He's not exactly my boy."

Max held his gaze for a moment too long. Andre let him. Their breath mixed in a hot cloud. Max cleared his throat and sat up, brushing snow from his calves. "Good-looker, though."

Andre pushed himself up to standing. "Feel free. I don't fuck students. Now shall we go back? I could use a cup of coffee."

Max stood. "I don't fuck anyone down here on the ice."

Andre's eyebrows rose. "I would have thought sex would warm you up in the cold. You strike me as a man who takes his pleasures where he finds them."

Max began walking toward the camp. "It's a job thing. Divers aren't faggots."

Andre took a few quick steps and caught up. "I dive."

Max shook his head. "You dive, but you're not a diver. No offense. It's not the same thing."

The wind was behind them on the way back, making it easier to talk. "Because real divers are irresponsible, womanizing drunks like your friends?"

"Something like that." Max picked up the pace.

Andre kept at it. "It's a sexual preference, not a personality profile."

Max stopped and turned toward him. "You think I don't know that? I've known who I am since I was a kid. Maybe I don't have your fancy education, but I'm not dumb, and I'm not chicken. I don't come out down here because I know what it's cost me in the past, and I like this job. Get off my case."

Andre looked puzzled. "You wouldn't lose your job. Sexual preference is contractually protected."

Max snorted and started walking. "Contractually protected. Like that matters. It must be nice to live in your world."

He trudged back toward camp, keeping a few feet in front of Andre the whole way. The guy was fucking dangerous. If Max didn't stay away from him, he might lose his job and lose the underwater wonderland he dreamed of all winter long.

Henrick scowled at Max as he entered the warming hut. His hands shook as he held his mug. "This much trouble over *pissen*?"

Andre stepped inside, squeezing past Max to stand before Henrick. He spoke quietly in German.

Henrick seemed irritated to Max, but what did he know? With all those consonants, German always sounded angry. Except it didn't coming from Andre.

Henrick turned toward Max, his back straight. "I am sorry for the trouble I caused. But if you had given better directions, it would not have happened."

Andre's German did sound sharp that time.

Henrick shrugged and looked away.

Max reached past him and snagged two coffee cups. He filled one for himself and passed the other to Andre. "Next time take a pee jar into the tent. You wouldn't believe the paperwork involved with accidental death."

Henrick frowned at him.

Max grinned.

Chief Jackson poked his head in the door. "If you ladies are done with your coffee klatch, we can get going with the morning program."

"Yes, sir." Max saluted him with his coffee cup. "We'll be right there."

* * *

Sunset had begun when Max called his group together for the last exercise in Happy Camper School, a simulated search for a lost colleague during a whiteout. Everyone clustered around the warming hut. Max produced a length of rope and staked one end near the hut.

"The wind can whip up a lot of snow. The general rule is that you don't go outside during whiteout conditions. But not everyone follows the rules." He caught Henrick's eye. Henrick had the balls to scowl back. "We're going to give you a feel for what a search would be like in a blizzard."

He held up the unattached end of the rope. "You've probably read stories about farmers tying a rope from the house to the barn when they went out to milk the cows during a snowstorm. Going outside without some way of finding your way back is suicidal, which means you're all going to hang on to some part of this rope."

He passed it to the woman standing closest to him. She grasped a section and passed the rest along. When everyone had a hand on the rope, Max held up a stack of white five-gallon buckets with eyes and mouths drawn on them in crude black marker. "Smitty and I will pass these out. Put them over your head and presto, instant whiteout. As soon as you're all bucketed, I'll send Smitty out to be the victim. When you find him, we're done. If you don't find him within the hour, we'll declare him dead and head back to the station. Any questions?"

They passed out the buckets. Max placed Smitty in a spot forty-five degrees north of the hut. It didn't really matter. They wouldn't find him. They never did. The point of the exercise was to scare people away from going out into a blizzard alone. Max thought it might be overkill with this group. They'd already experienced the adrenaline rush of a lost colleague. The simulation couldn't possibly match the emotional charge of the morning's search.

The point man on the rope was a big guy, a diesel mechanic who'd described himself as a philosopher during introductions. He led them out in a straight line for a few steps. Predictably, they began to drift off course. Max sat on an overturned bucket, out of reach of the rope, and watched. Soon the line had disintegrated into a half circle, a cluster, and eventually a huddle. He heard muffled discussion. A tall figure exchanged places with the mechanic. He spoke for a long time, gesticulating assertively, despite the fact that none of his listeners could see his hands.

The new leader pulled away, and Max realized he was walking backward. Even from this distance, he knew that walk. Andre was fucking irritating, but even so, Max liked to watch him move. The entire line of people followed, also walking backward. This was a novel technique. The line stretched out to its limit, stopped by a shout from the big mechanic, who now stood at the hut end of the rope, his feet braced, facing the line. Andre began stepping sideways, shouting as he did and continuing to lean back against the rope. The next person in line stepped and shouted, as did the one after that, and the whole line inched in a slow arc to the west.

When they were horizontal to the hut, the mechanic jerked hard on the line. His pull was echoed up the rope. As they felt it, each person stopped and tugged the person behind them. When the signal reached Andre, the group reversed course, making another plodding arc to the east. Max had never seen anything like it. It was brilliant. By facing backward, each link in the line was able to hold a tension they might have lost facing forward. Andre dictated their movement, and the anchor man could feel when the line had gone far enough in one direction and signal the group to change.

The line inched toward Smitty. A small figure touched him and gave a wild whoop. Word went up and down the line, and gradually the mechanic pulled them back in, reeling in Smitty along with the rest of them. Max shook his head in amazement and went off to congratulate the team.

Chapter Four

It always amazed Max how quickly McMurdo devolved into an adult version of middle school. Maybe it was the pressure of seeing the same people every day, the lack of privacy, or the institutional atmosphere, but he always suspected it had to do with mealtimes. Cafeteria cliques dissolved and reformed within days of the beginning of a season, the new configurations holding fast until the next change. Which, in this case, would be the October influx of mainbody folk.

For Annie's sake, he would have been welcome with the mechanics and maintenance workers at her winter-overs table. But there the conversation fluctuated between silence and metaphysical ramblings that he couldn't follow. McMurdo Station may be the only place on earth where all the janitors read Kant and car jockeys discussed string theory. While Max was equally uninterested in Bones and Smitty's pussy-hunting discussions, at least he understood the vocabulary.

Andre and Henrick seemed to have found their place among the other data types—the computer programmers— while Chief Jackson ate with the NSF station manager and the winter operations officer. As head of maintenance and lead mechanic, Annie could have found a chair at that table. But authority figures weren't her thing.

WinFly—the two months between the end of Antarctic winter in August and the beginning of the austral summer research season in October—was all about preparation. A busy but laid-back time compared to summer, when the population of McMurdo swelled to over a thousand and the pace picked up to frantic.

Max, Smitty, and Bones started the preparations by testing and cataloging dive gear and the marine sampling equipment. A couple of nights a week they headed to Gallagher's Pub for boilermakers and pool. Smitty kept up a running flirtation with the bartender. Bones claimed he was waiting for fresh meat to drop from the sky in October, but Max suspected he'd struck out all around with the available WinFly women. Henrick showed up one dark Thursday night and lost three games—and twenty bucks—to Smitty's pool shark ways. When Max asked casually where his professor was, Henrick shrugged.

The full moon came, and Max declined all recreational invitations. He and Annie had a standing date. One of the only things she ever needed from another human being was babysitting when she flew, which she did on solstices, the equinox, and every full moon. In a ritual that was part new age spirituality and part therapy, she lit a candle, settled herself on a meditation cushion, and slipped a tab of LSD onto her tongue.

Max lay on his bunk, DVDs stacked beside him, with an earbud tuned to the sound track of an old Bruce Willis movie playing on his laptop in one ear, and the other ear open in case Annie needed help. The dregs of a bottle of gin called to him, but he ignored the temptation. While she tripped, getting drunk was out of the question. It was the only promise she'd ever extracted from him—no drinking when she dropped. A night of sobriety every now and then wasn't much to ask.

Once, he'd walked her to Observation Hill, thinking she'd be awed by the sight of Mount Erebus, the ocean, and the Transantarctic Mountains sparkling in the midnight sun. Her eyes had focused instead on the dirty smudge of McMurdo below, and she'd wept. Later she told him it had looked to her like a dark metal spider burrowing into the continent, laying poisonous eggs that would hatch and destroy the last pristine place on earth. She'd been depressed for days. After that he left her alone, cocooned within the curtains of filmy Indian tapestry that cascaded in folds around her bed.

Annie had smiled at Max before arranging the curtains around herself. "It's going to be fine. No monsters tonight."

Good. Because Annie had monsters. One night a few years ago, Max had woken to her scream. He bolted to her bed and held her for hours as she thrashed and cried. In the morning, bleary-eyed and shaken, she'd told him how she'd earned her scars. "I was standing in the kitchen doorway, holding my baby brother, and watching Mom cook meth in our kitchen. She had a big pot simmering on the stove. There were jars and boxes and five-gallon jugs of chemicals all over the counter, and the air was choked with the smell of ammonia and rotten eggs. My middle brother, Johnnie, came running around the corner from the living room, bouncing a basketball. He lost control of the ball. It hit the stove. The sound…it was low and windy, like God exhaling. And the heat. I woke in the hospital with my head bandaged, the left side of my face still on fire with pain. Everybody was dead." She had stared at Max, her eyes huge with tears. "My baby brother… I was holding him on my right side, kissing his cheek."

Monsters. Max's own childhood hadn't been exactly a picnic. His mom was a drunk and his dad violent. Bad things had happened, but none of his memories began with either of them in the kitchen cooking meth.

So some trips were hard. But most times she lay quietly, sometimes humming or singing, playing with her fingers or giggling into the dark, and when she woke, she said things like, "The world is a web of love" and "God smiles as she watches us dream."

Max hit Play and watched Bruce Willis's lopsided grin as he fired bullets into bad guys. Wouldn't life be easier if that was all it took?

* * *

Smitty and Bones had been sent to lend a hand to the crew working on the new ice runway. Max sat on an overturned five-gallon bucket beside a bin of jumbled dry suit components, sorting and pairing dive gloves.

Chief Jackson entered the equipment room, slung an empty duffel off a shelf, and tossed it to Max. "Pack up three sets of gear. Dubois and his student want to get their sampling project started."

"Now?" Max grimaced.

Chief Jackson pulled down another two duffels. "Dubois says he needs to collect some samples left on the sea bottom over winter and set up new gear. You need to get going. The weather should hold for the rest of the week, but it might turn nasty by the weekend. It will take you a few days to set up camp. The dive hut is still out where they left it in March, which will save you a day or two."

"You want me to go with them? Couldn't Smitty or Bones go?" Max gestured toward the bin of gloves he had been sorting, like it offered up an excuse. The last thing he needed was to be out on the ice again with Andre Dubois.

Chief Jackson shook his head. "It'll only be Dubois and his student. It's my job to send along a safety diver to make sure they don't kill themselves. Smitty and Bones are good divers, and I'd use them if this was midseason and the whole research team was out there. But under the circumstances, that would be irresponsible. You're available, you have twice their training, and you know how to handle yourself in an emergency." He nodded toward the pile of dry suit bits and pieces. "The boys can get these sorted. It doesn't exactly require your unique skill set."

Max picked up the duffel bag. He sighed. "I'll pack up my gear, but you'd better get them down here to try stuff on. I don't want to have to come back if the long underwear is too small."

Footsteps sounded in the hallway outside. Jackson grinned and looked at his watch. "Right on time."

Andre entered first, shaking the Chief's hand and giving Max a quick nod. Henrick followed, his bulk making the room seem even smaller than it was.

"I'll leave you to it." Jackson spun on his heels. At the locker room doorway he turned back. "Your snowcat leaves first thing in the morning. I've got the kitchen putting a box of food together now." And with that he was gone.

Henrick surveyed the equipment room. "I thought you would have more here with all your American money."

"We have everything we need." Max looked him over, took a pair of thermal underwear from a shelf, and handed it to him. "Extra large, right? And I'm guessing you're about a forty-four-inch chest. Take the DUI dry suit on the end and try it on."

Henrick reached for the suit. He looked around the room. "Where should I change?"

Max shrugged. "Here if you want. Doesn't bother me."

He grimaced. "I'll be back." He rushed out the door.

Max raised his eyebrows and looked at Andre. "I thought Germans were supposed to be comfortable in the nude."

Andre shrugged. "Henrick knows I'm gay. Maybe that's why he's shy. It is better than if he displayed himself for us, yes?" His gaze held Max's. "I would expect you to understand when someone wants to hide."

Max bit back a retort and turned to the wall of clothing.

"Medium and extra long," Andre supplied. "In case you have forgotten."

Max handed him the underwear, the picture of Andre's naked torso suddenly vivid in his imagination. "No, I haven't forgotten."

Andre's mouth curved in something like a smile. "I haven't either." He cocked his head at Max. "I would rather not run down the hall like a frightened child. If you don't mind, I'll change here."

Max nodded. He turned to face the line of dry suits, pretending to paw through them, but instead listening to the rustle of Andre's clothing. He could almost feel the heat from Andre's body, close to his in the small room. It wasn't like Andre was getting naked. He'd have on his underwear, maybe an undershirt. Would he wear briefs or boxers? Briefs, Max decided. Europeans wore briefs. If Max turned around, would he see Andre's ass cheeks outlined in tight briefs? Trying to get the image of Andre's ass out of his head, Max shifted himself, grateful for the loose fit of his nylon overalls. Christ, what was he, twelve?

"And the dry suit?" Andre's voice was soft. Max shivered despite himself.

Max riffled through the suits until he found the right size and turned to see Andre, lean and beautiful in the black fleece thermal jumpsuit. Max watched him climb into the orange rubber suit that would keep him dry in the polar sea. Andre grimaced as he pushed his arms through and stood.

Max studied the fit of the suit. "It will pucker up around you at depth, but there's no getting around that, unless you want to gain thirty pounds."

Andre shrugged. "I'm used to that. It is why I prefer a wet suit."

"In twenty-eight-degree water you'd change your mind about that. Let me check the arms." He could have simply pulled on the cuffs to check the length, but instead he ran his hands down Andre's arms from shoulder to wrist.

Andre raised an eyebrow and asked softly, "What do you think? Does it fit?"

Max nodded, his mouth dry. His eyes focused on Andre's mouth as he continued speaking.

Andre's lips turned up in a slight smile. "I did like kissing you."

Max blinked at him, startled.

Andre's face hardened. "You don't remember even that? Fine. It never happened."

Max opened his mouth to speak, but the door flew open, and Henrick strode in.

"This is too small." He patted his rubberized chest. "Do you have anything bigger?"

Andre picked up his clothing and strode from the room.

* * *

Getting time to oneself in Antarctica was surprisingly difficult. A solitary soul might jump at the opportunity to sit alone beside a hole in the ice, watching for seals or people to appear. Always up for an opportunity to get away from the bustle of the station, Annie volunteered to provide general support and drive the snowcat, an orange box on tractor treads that really did look like a toy.

Annie pulled up to the dive locker building in the early morning dark. Max was already there, piling equipment on a pallet beside the door. Surviving the frigid waters beneath the Antarctic ice required an enormous amount of equipment. Dry suits, air tanks, and weight belts, of course, as well as specially designed nonfreezing regulators, two for each diver plus some spares since the extreme conditions were notoriously hard on them, a portable air compressor, pony bottles of emergency air, and the equipment needed for drilling or melting holes in the ice. Andre and Henrick showed up with crates of sampling equipment. By the time they finished loading the gear, cramming in a couple of huge tents, camping gear, and food, the twelve-person vehicle felt very crowded.

They started their slow crawl across the ice through the dark. At ten miles per hour, the trip took a long time. The plan was to arrive at the tip of Ross Island before the sun set, so that they'd have light for setting up camp. The noise of the snowcat limited conversation. Max watched the frozen landscape pass and avoided Andre's gaze. They hadn't spoken since the day before.

If it came up again, Max had no idea what he'd say to the man about their kiss. Kisses? Make-out session? Hell, exactly what had happened between them? He could almost remember someone at the bar with him, someone tall. But after that it was a big black hole. Not an unfamiliar feeling, but usually he could rationalize that whatever happened in that blackness, he was better off not remembering. But kissing Andre? That was something Max wished he could recall.

Of course, maybe nothing had happened, and Andre was jerking his chain. Self-righteous prick. Except there was that look of hurt when he'd realized Max couldn't remember. Andre wasn't used to being forgotten, and he didn't like it.

Max stole a glance at him. He seemed to be dozing, his eyes closed and body loose as they jostled across the ice. Henrick, beside him, was trying to read, his brow furrowed with concentration. Max shifted his gaze to the window again. It was going to be a very long week.

Chapter Five

Henrick looked a little green as he stared at the six-foot-long tunnel of ice they would have to pass through to dive in the sea below. It had taken them most of two days to get everything set up. Now that the hole was drilled, it was time to get wet.

Max was determined to get through the checkout dives before the light completely disappeared. "I'll go down first, and you can join me, Henrick. We'll do some simple checks, make sure you're comfortable, that your buoyancy is good, that you can find the safety hole, in case a seal is occupying this one, and give you a chance to get your breathing under control. It will be colder than the ice diving you've done before because seawater has a lower freezing point."

Henrick frowned at him. "I have a master's degree in oceanography and another in biochemistry. I am aware of the freezing point of seawater."

This guy was getting on his nerves. Max crossed his arms over his chest. "What you can't know until you've been down in it is how that will impact your diving. In my experience, which I'll admit I didn't get in a classroom, people have a tendency to suck down air during their first dive under this ice."

Annie hit him on the back, the slap against his rubber skin loud in the tiny hut. "Stop it, both of you. Hold on to your peckers. I don't want to have to help you get in and out of these things again. We can get the measuring stick out later."

Andre's laugh was explosive. "Nicely put." He turned toward Henrick. "Let us postulate that Mr. Conway has more experience than either of us diving in these particular conditions."

Henrick mumbled something under his breath and cast a hostile glance toward Max. Great. A big bad diver tantrum.

Max sighed and started again. "Let's finish getting suited up. Um, Dr. Dubois, can you help Henrick with his tank and gloves?"

Andre's mouth curved into a slight smile. "Of course, Mr. Conway."

Annie looked from one to the other and shook her head. Max pulled his hood on and bent to sling his tank over one shoulder. She helped him with the other strap, handed him his mask, and snapped his gloves over the cuffs of his suit. He tested his two regulators and watched Henrick do the same.

"Okay?"

Henrick nodded. Max slipped into the hole and, with a wave, began to descend. The first dive of the season always felt like sliding into his real life.

The wall of ice glistened around him as he cleared his ears, let more air out of his dry suit, and drifted down. He tensed against the icy cold as it bit into the exposed flesh of his lips, concentrating on his breath—long, slow, Darth Vader inhales and exhales. Bubbles filled the ice tube as he exhaled, and he was through the tunnel and out into the deep blue of the Antarctic sea.

Max moved away from the hole and checked out the area in a lazy circle. The ice above made a crystalline ceiling. Off to the west, the round window of the safety hole shone brightly. Weightless, suspended fifty feet above the ocean floor, Max relaxed into his skin.

Fins appeared, followed by knees. The crinkling of Henrick's dry suit around his calves told Max that he had let out too much air and was sinking fast. Max grabbed the safety line with one hand and with the other hooked Henrick by the tank as he sank past him. Henrick's eyes were wide in his mask. Max tapped his own chest, the safety line swaying as he did. Henrick stared at him for a long moment before making the adjustment. Air hissed into his suit. He floated up, hit his head on the bottom of the ice, let air out, and came to hover next to Max, who held Henrick's gaze until the wild, panicked look subsided.

Max let go of the rope and gestured for Henrick to take it. He made Henrick go through a sequence of inflating and deflating his dry suit. Wherever Henrick had done his qualifying ice dives, it hadn't prepared him for the feeling of being in the polar dark and cold. Max glanced at the safety hole. He had planned for them to swim to it, but Henrick's air might not hold. Max checked Henrick's gauge. Christ. He had to have been panting to use it up that fast. It looked like Max would be babysitting this one for a few more dives. He gave the thumbs-up gesture and followed Henrick up the ice tube.

From a few feet underwater, Max watched Annie helping Henrick haul himself out of the hole and onto the ice. Max pointed at Andre, making sure he nodded before Max began his own descent. If Andre was as awkward in the water as his student, Max was in trouble.

But Andre spiraled out of the ice tube with perfect control, his trajectory taking him in exactly the same kind of circle with which Max had emerged. Andre stopped smoothly in front of him. Together they swam to the safety hole. Andre looked up, nodded, and glanced down at the seafloor below. He turned to Max, his eyebrows up and thumb pointed down. Andre wanted to enjoy his dive.

Max grinned to himself and nodded. Their eyes locked as they descended. It felt like a dance. As they neared the bottom, they turned in unison to skirt the ocean floor. Andre pointed to a patch of anemones, bright red against the black and brown of the surrounding environment. A jellyfish floated past, swimming upward with an elegant bellows' breath. Max checked Andre's pressure gauge and smiled again. This man was not going to give him problems underwater. Max watched the smooth flow of Andre's legs as his fins scissored through the water—sleek and graceful. They swam slowly across the bottom for a few more minutes. Max checked his dive watch. It was time to go up. He patted Andre on the arm and gave the thumbs-up gesture. Andre nodded.

They looked up to see two Weddell seals tumbling around each other ten feet over their heads. Andre bounced in the water. He must have caught his breath and the air in his lungs had buoyed him. Slowly he drifted back down, still watching the huge seals play. Just as Max thought he'd need to steer them to the safety hole, the seals moved on, and the two of them ascended. He let Andre pass into the ice tunnel first and watched as he waved Annie away and gracefully hoisted himself onto the ice. Max followed. He might have to spend a week or more teaching young Henrick to dive, but Andre was as good as anyone Max had ever worked with. Max gazed at Andre standing beside Annie, looking tall and as smooth and beautiful as a seal. He might not cause Max trouble underwater, but topside, that was a different thing.

Max pulled off his mask and hood.

Andre did the same, his dark hair falling in damp curls. "That was beautiful. The seals, they were marvelous. Weddells, yes? Not leopards, certainly."

Max nodded. "You'll see a lot of Weddells around here. Leopard seals are rare, but when you see them it's dramatic."

Annie squatted beside Andre and helped him shrug off his tank. "Wasn't it a leopard seal that got that diver a few years ago? Took her down a couple hundred feet and killed her?"

Max opened his mouth to answer, but Andre jumped in. "Any large animal can be dangerous if you're not careful. There have been very few accidents involving leopard seals and none with Weddells. Am I right?" He looked at Max.

"Yeah. Although leopards are huge and have really big teeth, which can scare the shit out of you." He glanced at Annie. "Speaking of scared, how's Henrick?"

She grimaced. "He's gone to change. I don't think he liked it down there."

Max yanked off his gloves and tossed them onto the ice floor. "Yeah. That's what I thought. We'll be fine here, if you want to take off. I think we can get this stuff rinsed and put away on our own." He looked at Andre for confirmation.

He was nodding. "Of course. You have been very helpful, but perhaps you have something you'd rather be doing."

She laughed. "Rather than handle your cold, wet equipment? Hardly. But I would like to check on the weather. Last I looked, there was a storm coming. We should get the camp ready."

Max nodded. "Get Henrick to help you string lines between the tents and the hut in case we get a whiteout. And maybe someone could put on a pot of water for tea or cocoa. We'll be damned cold by the time we're done here."

"Sure thing." She grinned and spun on her heel.

Leaving Max and Andre alone in the warming hut.

"It did not go well with Henrick?" Andre was peeling out of his dry suit.

Max dumped his weight belt and stood. "My guess is he's claustrophobic, and the ice tube freaked him out. 'Cause the only other explanation is he's never been in a dry suit before, and that can't be true."

Andre shook his head. "The university has a qualification course for polar diving. Everyone, myself included, has to go through it before being allowed to participate in this research project."

"But that's not where you learned to dive." Max unzipped his suit.

Andre stepped out of his, shook it, and hung it next to Henrick's. "My father was a big fan of Jacques Cousteau. All our vacations were spent diving. Usually in warmer water than this."

"But you're fine under ice." Max hung up his suit and began unscrewing his regulator from his tank.

Andre shrugged, his attention on his tanks. "Most of my diving these days is for research. I have winter field sites under frozen lakes, underneath piers, in caves. They are not so different from this."

Max straightened, his hands on his hips. "It's my job to make sure everyone dives safely."

Andre looked up from his tank and nodded.

Max took a deep breath and blew it out. "He's not up to it."

Andre shrugged. "So I'll go on my own."

Max shook his head. "Not happening. I'd lose my job, and you'd have your Antarctic dive permit pulled. You have two choices. I can work with him for a week or so, see if he can push through that panic. Or I'm your other diver."

Andre stood, his arms crossed over his chest. "You don't know what you're doing. You'll wreck the site and ruin hundreds of thousands of dollars' worth of research."

Max shrugged. His feet were getting cold and his patience thin. "Maybe. But as long as I'm the safety diver, I'm in charge of everything that happens in this hut. I can and I will ground this whole operation if I think you're endangering yourself or Henrick."

Andre scowled at him.

Max hefted his tank onto a cart. He'd haul them out to the compressor for a topping off later. He turned back to Andre, his hands spread. "I'm trainable. There isn't much that can be done underwater that I haven't tried, and I haven't ruined anyone's research or construction site or nuclear cooling tower. I've sneaked into some hostile places without getting noticed or shot at. I've—"

"Stop." Andre held up a hand. "I'm not interested in your résumé. You can work with Henrick later. For now, while I would rather have a trained scientist work with me, if that's not possible, so be it."

Max grinned, delighted at the thought of spending a week underwater with a competent dive buddy rather than sitting up top watching for bubbles. "Okay. Tomorrow morning you can show me what we're doing, and we'll start as soon as it's light."

Andre considered him for a long moment. "I need to ask something of you. I don't mean to be offensive, but I'm afraid you will take it that way."

Max's grin faded. "What." It came out more like a bark than a word.

Andre bit his lip and looked into Max's eyes. "This really is important, the research. Can I count on your sobriety?"

Max jerked back like he'd been slapped. "Can you… Shit. Just because I take a drink or two doesn't mean….Yes, you can count on my sobriety. Now hand me that bucket. We need to get these things rinsed down."

* * *

The storm hit as they were finishing dinner—canned stew Henrick had heated while the others strung safety lines, checked tent holdings, and made sure everything was battened down securely. The wind slapped the sides of the survival tent with a howl, made the fabric flutter, and drowned out the steady hiss of the propane heater.

The camp consisted of a large survival tent with one side dedicated to cooking and eating and four cots clustered in the other. A separate, much smaller "outhouse" tent contained the chemical toilet and served as a supply cabinet. Both tents were only feet from the diving hut, a tin box that could be dragged over a dive hole. Propane heaters kept the temperature in all three structures above freezing, but general field conditions were cold. Even without a windstorm.

Annie rinsed her dish, kicked off her boots, crawled into her sleeping bag, and turned away from the group to face the wall.

"Would anyone else like some tea?" Andre sloshed water into the kettle and put it on the camp stove.

"I'm going to bed." Henrick's shoulders slumped as he walked toward his cot. Andre had taken him outside before dinner, and Max assumed he'd told Henrick that he wouldn't be diving this trip. Given the poor guy's terror in the dive hole, it should have been a relief, and maybe it was, but it also had to feel like a slap down.

In the Navy, Max had experienced every type of leader imaginable. Some believed in public reprimand as a way to ensure that their underlings behaved better in the future. Others took you aside for a private talk, like Andre must have done. In Max's opinion, those were the supervisors who got the most out of their troops. Henrick would soon bounce back to his arrogant self, and once they returned to the station, there'd be time for Max to help him get over the ice tunnel heebie-jeebies.

The kettle whistled, and Andre poured water into two mugs. He handed one to Max, who dumped in a package of hot chocolate and dug a flask out of his duffel. Andre's eyebrows rose.

Max poured a shot into his mug. He held up the flask. "Not for getting drunk. It'll help me sleep. Want some?"

Andre shook his head. He smiled sadly into his tea. "How long is the storm supposed to last?"

"At least a couple days." The smell of chocolate filled his nostrils. His first swig was hot and smooth, the brandy warming him all the way down. "It won't matter once we're underwater. We'll have about six hours of relative daylight tomorrow. We should be able to get in several good dives."

Andre leaned back in his chair, his long legs stretched toward the stove. "It's not very deep. I'd need to check the dive tables, but I think we could go a long time if we had enough air."

Max took another swallow and shook his head. "Your feet start to ache in the cold after half an hour, and your hands get useless not long after that. We'll need to come up and get warm in between."

Andre played with the string on his tea bag. "You said something about diving under hostile conditions. Were you a military diver?"

"Joined the navy as soon as I turned eighteen. They taught me to dive." He chuckled. "I was still pretty green when I signed up to try out for the SEALs. Got through Hell Week, after which I nearly drowned a few times during the underwater training."

"Hell Week?" Andre smiled softly. "I think I've had a few of those."

Max shook his head, stretching his own legs out. His feet almost touched Andre's. "I hope not like Hell Week during BUD/S—five and a half days of grueling physical hardship with virtually no sleep. I never want to do that again."

"Did you like it, the military? You still keep your hair short." Andre tugged on one of his own curls. They looked soft, long but not like a hippie-freak. Andre's hair feathered around his face, brushed the sides of his cheeks, and touched his collar in the back.

Max ran a hand over his own bristly head. "I'm in the water a lot. This is easier."

Andre smiled at him over his mug. "It's a good look for you. But you didn't answer my question."

"Did I like it?" Max shrugged. "Sure, parts of it. Other parts sucked."

"The diving? That's what you liked?"

Max snorted. "Diving is only part of what SEALs do. Afghanistan's landlocked. Toward the end of my last tour, the only diving I was getting was out of a plane."

Andre stared into his tea. "Was it awful? Fighting there?"

Max grimaced. "People always ask that. It's right up there with 'did you kill anyone?' What am I supposed to say? It was great? Yeah, I really loved seeing my friends blown into bloody pieces. It was like fucking fireworks."

Andre contemplated Max. "Is that why you left?"

Max drained his mug. "I'm gonna check on the heater in the dive hut. We can't afford to have those regulators freeze." He stood, rinsed his mug, and stole a look at his duffel. Another shot would hit the spot. He closed his eyes and gritted his teeth. Not out on the ice, no matter what. Besides, if he didn't stick with his one-shot-a-night ration, he'd run out before they got home. That thought sent a chill through him, and he shivered. When he opened his eyes, he saw Andre watching him.

Max shrugged on his coat and stormed out of the tent. Jesus Christ. Fucking puritan. Fucking idiot. Did he like the military? What the fuck kind of question was that? The wind hit him with a slap. One hand on the safety line, he bowed his head and trudged toward the dive hut, blinking away the nightmare vision of that last convoy, the one that got the kid from Brooklyn, the ambush that only happened because Max hadn't been paying enough attention. He shook his head. If he kept this up, he'd be draining that flask before midnight. Max turned his attention to the regulators. Having them freeze was life threatening enough. He didn't need to remember a time when he'd had a band of brothers, or the point when they all disappeared.

By the time he returned, everyone was in bed. Max doused the lights and crawled into the only empty cot. Right next to Andre.

* * *

Max woke to the smell of brewing coffee. The wind had died down and was playing gently with the fabric of the tent. He poked his head out the top of the sleeping bag and opened his eyes. Andre sat on a camp chair, a mug in one hand and a book in the other. He glanced up at the sound of Max sliding out of his bag.

"Good morning." He gestured toward the kitchen area where Henrick was cracking eggs into a bowl. "It appears our Henrick has taken on the job of camp cook. He makes excellent coffee, although it may be too strong for your American tastes."

Max grunted. "The stronger the better for me." He looked around. "Where's Annie?"

Henrick gestured toward the door. "She was leaving as I got up. She said we should meet her in the dive hut when we're ready."

Max nodded. That sounded like Annie.

"I think she likes her privacy." Andre smiled. "I don't blame her. I didn't expect Antarctica to be this crowded myself."

Max smiled, sliding into his boots. "We all get to know each other way too well down here. Wait until midsummer. You'll have people telling you their deep dark secrets and crying in the hallways. Something about our enforced togetherness, I guess."

Andre cocked his head, his eyes half-lidded and challenging. "I don't imagine you share your secrets."

Max felt a rush of heat at his suggestive tone. He shot a look at Henrick, who poured eggs into a fry pan, seemingly oblivious to the sudden escalation of tension in the room.

Max met Andre's gaze and shook his head. "You know the old SEAL saying, 'It's all mind over matter. If you don't mind, it don't matter.'" He pulled on his parka and stepped out of the tent. He had a pee jar under his cot, but the last thing he was going to do at that very moment was pull out his dick in Andre's presence.

Chapter Six

Andre spread papers across the folding table they were using for everything from a kitchen counter to a work desk. He pointed to a map of the ocean bottom beneath them. Red marks dotted the map, GPS coordinates beside them. "There are twenty sites. The depths last March ranged from ten to twenty meters or about thirty to seventy feet by your dive tables. At each site we'll recover the sampling units we left to overwinter and replace them with fresh ones. I was not part of the team last year, but the notes indicate that with travel time, we should be able to accomplish everything we need to at a site in a single, thirty-minute dive." He glanced back at Henrick. "Maybe faster since we'll have someone up top who knows how to process the samples we deliver."

"How many deep sites?" Max leaned down to examine the map, careful not to brush against Andre.

"Three. Here, here, and here." Andre pointed to spots at the edge of the sampling zone.

Max straightened. "There's a big storm predicted for the end of the week. I'd like to be back in McMurdo before it hits. That gives us five days to do twenty dives."

"Twenty-one." Andre's voice was firm. "Our first dive today will be for training purposes." Max looked at him with raised eyebrows. Andre continued, "You understand about checkout dives."

Behind them Henrick snickered.

Max glanced toward him, then back at Andre. "Okay, twenty-one dives in five days." He consulted the plastic dive tables that let him calculate how long a diver could stay at a given depth without risking the bends. "Four dives a day makes sense to me. We can do thirty minutes down, take a break to warm up, go back down again, take a long enough lunch to get the nitrogen out of our systems, and do it all again in the afternoon. But we'll need to plan carefully to get five dives into one day."

Andre glanced at the dive tables. "Why not use a dive computer? It would be easier, and we could get more time on the bottom."

"They freeze up." Max jotted a few numbers on a scrap of paper. "All right. We'll do four a day and five the last. By that time we should have our routine down, and we might be able to shave a few minutes off each dive. It will also be light longer. Today we'll be lucky to get through four without lights. Okay, show me what we're doing."

* * *

As he slid into the water behind Andre, Max realized how much he was looking forward to the next few days. All winter, during the off-season, he worked as a commercial diver in places like San Diego harbor, where visibility was low and the work mundane, and he dreamed about this cold blue world. Diving here was completely different from the industrial sludge sites where he worked the rest of the year or the armed dives he'd done in Somalia, Yemen, and Iraq before the unit transferred to Afghanistan. If there was a heaven, which Max very much doubted, it would be exactly this color of blue. It wasn't the same for Smitty, who'd been a scuba instructor in the Bahamas and was used to bright colors and abundant fish. He called the polar sea a desert, which it probably was. But to Max it was a chance to dive in clear waters where visibility ranged up to three hundred feet. And while tiny, shrimplike krill and scuttling crabs were more abundant than fish, where else could you swim with penguins?

And there was Andre, eyes bright behind his mask as Max emerged beneath the hole. Maybe he felt it too, the pull of cold blue water as boundless as the sky. Max signaled okay, and Andre led him straight down to an unmarked spot. He buried a small square sampling unit, floated backward, and gestured for Max to retrieve it. Max pushed the plastic core tube over the square, dug through the sediment, pulled it up, placed it carefully in the plastic sampling bag, and handed the resulting package to Andre. Who shook his head violently, disassembled everything, reburied the unit with exaggerated gestures, and packaged it back up, signaling to Max what he had done wrong. And made him do the whole thing five times before he gestured for them to go up.

Max dragged himself out of the hole, cast off his mask, hood, and gloves, and gratefully accepted the hot mug of tea Annie offered. He turned to Henrick. "Your boss is tough."

Henrick smirked. "He's used to working with the best."

Andre, who was wiggling his feet to warm them up, snorted. "You should have seen what Professor Hicks put us through before he allowed us to take over his project. Yes, Henrick?"

Henrick groaned. "By the end my fingers were freezing. I thought they might fall off. And that was along the coast near San Diego in summer. We were on surface-supplied air and stayed down for hours."

"So, you see, I was easy on you. Even so, I'll collect the samples and you carry them. If we really need you to collect, now you know how." Andre glanced at his watch. "Ready?"

Max nodded, handed Annie his cup, and climbed back into his gear. They slid down the tube.

* * *

Last dive of the day, and they were swimming back toward the dive hole. If he thought about it too much, Max would have had to admit that his toes ached with cold. He navigated toward the bright window of the safety hole, which was easier to spot from a distance than the main hole, darkened by the warming hut above.

Andre's touch on his arm was featherlight. Max turned. Andre pointed into the azure distance where the ghostly figure of an icefish swam toward them. Big-eyed, long-beaked, almost transparent, it wasn't a rare sight under the ice but an eerie one. Andre's grip tightened as a sleek shiver of flesh swooped down from near the surface and engulfed the fish. They watched the seal swim away, apparently heading for a barely visible crack in the ice.

Andre looked at Max, blinked twice as if to say *did you see that*, and waved them forward to the dive hole. Max followed, watching him move smoothly through the water, trying not to notice the cold in his feet or the warmth in his groin.

Henrick took the last of the samples from Max as he emerged from the hole. Max waved Annie away. She'd done more waiting than working during the day, always accompanied by Henrick. It must have been driving her crazy. Henrick disappeared with the samples, taking them to the main tent for processing.

Andre shrugged out of his tank and weight belt and stood grinning at Max. "What a way to end the day, yes?"

Max nodded. "Not good for the icefish, though."

He laughed. "I don't know. Probably didn't know what hit him. That might not be a bad way to die."

They worked in silence for a few minutes, rinsing and hanging up the equipment. Max climbed out of his dry suit, hung it, and counted the tanks. He'd need to run the compressor and top off all the tanks. Leaning against the hut wall, he watched Andre, considering the long line of him, lean even in layers of thermal underwear.

Max cleared his throat. "Look, I'm really sorry about that first night."

Andre paused. He stood very still for a moment, considering Max. He took a step toward him. "What are you sorry about, that you passed out before we could finish or that you don't remember what we did?"

Max swallowed, his heart pounding. When he spoke, his voice cracked. "Both, I guess."

Andre nodded, moving even closer. "As am I." His hand was cold as he touched Max's cheek. "You're so beautiful, a beautiful wreck. Perhaps this will jog your memory."

His lips grazed softly against Max's, and it felt like all the air left the room. Max wasn't used to having to tip his head back to kiss someone. Who was he kidding? There hadn't been much kissing in the past few years of anonymous sex.

Andre pulled back. "No? Maybe because it was more like this."

He pulled Max into a full-body kiss. Andre's mouth tasted familiar, like the rubber mouthpiece of the regulator and something else, something Max could almost remember. Andre's tongue pressed against Max's, insistent and hungry. His hand moved to Max's hip, and he pushed Max up against the hut wall. Max's body responded instantly, his hands cradling Andre's head, tunneling into his wet hair, pulling him closer.

Andre reached between them, brushing Max's cock through his clothing. Max gasped and arched into him. Andre stroked hard, the press of his erection poking into Max's thigh. Suddenly Andre let go, broke the kiss, and stepped back.

"Now you know both how it feels to kiss me and how I felt when you passed out." He turned and left the hut.

Max stared after him, his cock still throbbing. His lips felt bruised, and his ego hurt. He knocked his head against the hut wall. He didn't need this. Not here. Not now. His mind filled with the memory of Andre standing at the edge of the bed, his torso bare and inviting. The kiss, the touch of Andre's hand, electric through the fleece.

Fuck.

How had he blacked out on something that good? And worse, passed out in the middle.

A sick feeling bloomed in the pit of his stomach, his old friend mortification. It warred with the pulse of his cock, which was supposed to be dead for the season but had sprung to life at Andre's touch. Max unzipped his fleece jumpsuit, dug through the layers to find his dick. It took only a few strokes and the memory of Andre pressing up against him. Max wiped his hand clean in disgust. Andre was at least half-right. He might not be beautiful, but he was a fucking wreck.

* * *

Max woke with a gasp. His heart pounded. He was sweating inside his bag. Same fucking dream as always. He'd been trapped underwater, his tank caught on something behind him. He couldn't move. His air stopped. Short. Nothing. Gone.

But the ice… had he been under the ice? He imagined his head hitting the ice, the echoing sound of it, and his panicked search for an exit. He breathed again. It was only a dream. Head pressed against his pillow, Max inhaled, exhaled, and reran the dream in his head, changing the ending until he slipped out of his tank and ascended, breaking the surface with a huge gulp of air.

The wind billowed against the tent. Someone turned over. Henrick? Annie coughed. Max inhaled the field-camp smell of stale cooking and wet socks. Andre lay close enough that Max could hear his breath. The sound traveled through him, cradling the dark pit of fear in his belly. Matching his own breathing to the rhythm of the man who slept nearby, Max let himself be carried back to sleep.

Chapter Seven

On the last day, they visited the final site with only twenty minutes left on their dive table. Max hadn't pushed tables since he took a summer job harvesting geoducks in Puget Sound. There the temptation to go beyond safe limits was strong, since more time at depth translated directly into money in the pocket. He'd been out drinking with some of the other divers when one of the guys started complaining about his knee and tingling in his toes. Over the next couple of days it got worse, until by the weekend the guy was thrashing with pain. That was followed by a trip to the emergency room, where the kid was assured that some time in a compression chamber, a ten-thousand-dollar hospital bill, and a couple of years out of the water would probably clear it up. Or maybe it wouldn't. They said he could end up with permanent damage. Only time would tell. The day before Max drove the kid in for treatment was the last time he pushed a table.

Fortunately, the site was near the dive hole, and they were able to get last year's sample out and a new unit in place with time to spare. To be safe, Max had them swim back near the surface, directly under the ice. Their bubbles floated and merged. They left a long trail of air clinging to the bottom of the ice as they swam. Far beneath, crabs scuttled across the ocean floor. Max drank it in. They'd leave in the morning, and it could be another month before he found himself able to enjoy a dive again. Once summer season started, there'd be plenty of bottom time. But until then he would spend his days cataloging and repairing equipment, only dipping below surface to coach Henrick. Of course, the good news was that once they were home he could take a good long drink, party with the guys. Maybe that would take his mind off the clean line of Andre's legs as they sliced through the water ahead of him. Or the memory of that kiss. Christ, the last thing he needed was to increase his metabolic rate underwater with half a tank's worth of air.

But the memory was stirring. And a repeat performance wasn't likely once they got back to the station. Privacy was in short supply at McMurdo, even shorter supply if Max intended to keep up his balancing act. If Max wanted more than a taste of Andre, it would have to be now, after Henrick and Annie disappeared into the main tent and the two of them were alone in the dive hut. He kicked forward, not willing to think beyond the next half hour and the pleasures it might bring.

Max crawled out of the hole, unsnapping his tank as he went. If he stripped out of his gear quickly, he could catch Andre unawares, sweep the man off his fucking feet. He waved Annie away impatiently. She raised her eyebrow, shrugged, and left the hut.

Henrick held his samples and nodded as Andre undid his buckles and clasps and talked. About the sites. And future plans. And talked some more. Henrick grunted, the notes he was mentally taking plastered across his face. Max watched them. Andre, the professor, instructing Henrick, the student, while Max, the thwarted lover, peeled out of his dry suit and rinsed saltwater off the gear.

"Do you mind finishing this up yourself?" Andre looked at Max. His eyes twinkled as he gestured toward the unrinsed gear. "I need to make some notes while it's all still fresh in my mind."

Max nodded. He felt like punching someone, but he wasn't sure who. Henrick for getting in the way, or Andre for making it happen? He growled, "I need to get this stuff packed up anyway."

In case he'd been wondering whether the lack of privacy had been an accident, Andre gave him one long, sultry look before striding away. Bastard. Fucking sexy bastard.

Max was still sulking later as he jostled his almost empty flask. Might as well finish it. No use taking any home. Turning his back on the others, he took a healthy slug and drained the remaining couple of shots into his hot chocolate. He closed his eyes, savoring the warmth of the brandy blooming in his chest. When he turned around, Andre was watching him. Well, fuck him. Or not, as the case may be.

* * *

The blizzard hit shortly after midnight. The wind rattled the tent, sounding like thunder. The temperature inside dropped a good ten degrees. Max buried his head in his bag and waited for morning, when the winds would die and they could drive out.

The wind howled through breakfast. Max's foray to the outhouse tent took him into full whiteout conditions. When he returned to the main tent, Annie was on the radio.

"The storm's a level two," she announced as she clicked off. "No travel today."

They all stared at her.

Andre spoke first. "Do they have an idea of how long this is going to last?"

Annie shrugged. "There's no weather station out here, so they can't be sure. Said we should be prepared to wait a couple of days, maybe a week."

Max's stomach fell. He felt a wave of panic. Only an effort of will kept him from glancing at his pack where the empty flask lay tucked beneath a layer of dirty underwear.

Andre's eyes were gentle as he gazed at Max. "We have enough food to last longer than that and plenty of snow to melt for water. We'll be fine."

Henrick laughed nervously. "Anyone have a deck of cards?"

Max's anger flared, and he snapped, "I'm not going to waste time on games. Come on, Henrick. Get suited up. No reason we can't dive. It's not storming underwater."

Henrick grimaced.

Andre nodded. "Good idea. You might as well get used to the diving conditions here. We'll be back in a month."

Fear washed across Henrick's face. Max softened. He'd been in plenty of scary spots and knew how that felt.

He patted Henrick's shoulder. "Come on. We'll ease in slow."

Andre stood. "I can help. We'll give Annie some time alone."

She beamed at him.

* * *

Max suited up while Andre helped Henrick on with his gear. Henrick was practically hyperventilating. Time hadn't improved his attitude toward the dive hole. It seemed to have gotten worse. At Max's direction, he sat on the edge of the hole, his feet inches above the water. From inside his mask, the whites of Henrick's eyes engulfed the pale blue of his irises. Max let his own mask dangle around his neck so that Henrick could see his face.

He touched Henrick's shoulder. The young man jumped.

Andre squatted beside him and patted his arm. Henrick looked at him. Andre took a deep breath and let it out, breathed in again, and Henrick followed, his breath echoing raspingly against the walls of the hut.

Max grabbed a coil of rope and knelt on the ice in front of him. "It's okay to be scared. We all get afraid sometimes.

The thing is that you've either got to walk away from all this or push through."

Henrick blinked several times. He glanced at Andre, at the hole in the ice, and back at Max. He nodded and cleared his throat. "I will do this."

Max smiled. "It's the tunnel through the ice that bothers you, right?"

Henrick shivered.

"Right. We have to get you used to it." Max uncoiled the rope and handed one end to Andre. "Dr. Dubois is gonna tie this rope to that hook in the wall. He'll make a real strong knot that won't come loose."

Andre took the rope and stood. He spoke softly as he walked to the spot Max had indicated. "Henrick calls me Andre. You might as well too."

Max smiled. He handed the other end of the rope to Henrick. "You'll hold on to this. That way you'll know which way is up and can climb back out whenever you need to. Do you understand?"

Henrick took the rope, clutching it tightly.

Max patted his knee. "You'll get through this. Now put your regulator in your mouth and jump in. You're not going all the way down. Stay in the hole and hang on to the rope. Tug twice if you want us to pull you up. Got it?"

Henrick nodded. He set the regulator in his mouth, and the hut filled with the whistle of his breath. With one last look at Andre, he slid into the water and slipped beneath the surface. Max leaned over the edge of the hole and watched the bobbing top of Henrick's head.

Max was concentrating hard. Andre's voice startled him. "You must have been good with frightened soldiers in the field."

Max snorted. "Hardly. No offense, but a SEAL would never let fear get him like that. He might feel terror like Henrick does, but no one would know."

Andre was silent for a long time. Max heard him shift closer. "You're proud of being a SEAL. Why did you leave? Was it because of something that happened on the battlefield?"

Max closed his eyes. And opened them to watch Henrick's bubbles bursting on the surface. Henrick was still breathing too hard. Max slipped his mask on and put a hand on his regulator in case he needed to go in after him. He considered not answering Andre, but undoubtedly he'd ask again.

Max took a deep breath. "No, not that. I got caught, pants around my ankles, with a civilian who gave the term embedded journalist a whole new meaning. Don't Ask, Don't Tell was still in force. My commander should have given me a dishonorable discharge. But my term was almost up, and like he said, 'There ain't no faggot SEALs and never have been.' I was transferred back to the States immediately with an honorable in exchange for not re-upping."

Andre gasped and pointed. The bubbles had stopped rising from Henrick. He must have passed out and let the regulator drop. His hand released, and he started to sink.

Max swore and plunged in after him, barely registering the slap of cold water against his face. He kept his gaze on Henrick, who slowly drifted down, a single bubble trapped between his mask and the crease of his nose. Max kicked hard. Grinding his jaw to relieve the pressure building in his ears, he pushed himself down beside Henrick, catching his arm as they emerged from the bottom of the ice tunnel. Max dived under him. Henrick's body pivoted above him, pulled in a slow pirouette by Max's grip on his arm. The bubble dislodged, and Max stared into Henrick's open, vacant eyes. Max pumped his legs as he pushed Henrick back up toward the air. Henrick's head broke the surface, and Max watched Andre's hands curl beneath his shoulders. Max felt Henrick being pulled away. He pushed from below, his fins hitting the ice wall with each kick, until his hands on Henrick's calves splashed out of the water.

Max let himself float in the ice tunnel for a few seconds as he caught his breath. By the time he got himself up out of the hole, Andre was administering CPR.

A minute passed. Another. Andre pressed, counted, breathed. Henrick sputtered, and Andre rolled him to his side. Water spilled from him in sharp coughs. Max met Andre's eyes, which were tearing with relief.

Henrick coughed again. Andre helped him as he struggled to sit. Henrick wiped his mouth and nose and looked at Max. "Can I try again?"

Max sat back on his heels and considered. He shrugged. Who was he to take away a man's dignity? He patted Henrick's shoulder. "We'll wait until after lunch."

Chapter Eight

Max rolled onto his back, trying to get comfortable, but sleep eluded him. The wind still howled around the tent. What he needed was.... He couldn't think about what he needed. Sitting up, he clicked on his penlight and looked around the crowded tent. There must be something he could do that wouldn't wake anyone. The beam reflected off the regulator that had frozen up their second day. Max eased his way out of bed. Maybe he'd get sleepy if he took it apart, checked all the fittings, and put it back together again. Anything was better than watching the tent walls billow.

Andre stirred in his bag. His whispered voice was muffled by the down. "There's a bag of candy in one of the crates. It might help."

"What?" Max stared at the lump on the cot next to his.

"Sugar will help with the withdrawal." Andre rolled over, pulling the sleeping bag tightly over his head. "Ease the craving and help you get some sleep."

Max scowled at him. Withdrawal? Craving? What did Andre think he was, a fucking alcoholic?

Now the empty flask was really calling to him. Fucking power of suggestion. Max waited until he heard slow, rhythmic breathing coming from Andre's cot before he went in search of candy.

* * *

By the end of the next day, Henrick could pass in and out of the ice tunnel without sucking down an entire air tank. He had a long way to go before Max could check him out but was making steady progress. Max, on the other hand, felt like shit. His head pounded, and food rumbled around in his stomach uncomfortably. Annie heated chicken soup. Andre offered to make him hot chocolate, but Max growled that he was coming down with something and wanted to be left the fuck alone. He crawled into his sleeping bag and pretended sleep.

Except his muscles kept twitching. He wanted to crawl out of his skin. He opened his eyes to see Andre whispering to Annie. She nodded, glanced at him sideways, clenching and unclenching her fists. He wanted to jump up out of his sleeping bag and slap both of them. Every muscle in his body needed to fight. Except he didn't want to move his pounding head.

Andre knelt beside his bed, holding out a couple of pills and a mug of cocoa. "I wish I had a sleeping pill to give you, but Benadryl's the best we have. Drink the chocolate. It might take the edge off what you're feeling."

"Since when is chocolate prescribed for the flu?" Max growled, sitting up to take the pills and the mug.

"You know it's not the flu," Andre whispered, resting his hand on Max's leg. "When was the last time you went two days without a drink?"

Max scowled. His hand shook as he threw back the pills and took a long sip of lukewarm chocolate. "You keep harping on that. I don't have a drinking problem. I must have picked up some bug at the base."

Andre dug in his pocket and produced a handful of hard candies. Dropping them in Max's lap, he stood. "Whatever you say."

Max slept fitfully, plagued by dreams of drowning, of fire, or of men and armored vehicles blown to pieces in front of him. Each time he woke drenched in sweat, Andre was wiping his forehead or offering him a drink of water or cocoa or candy. Max was too exhausted to fight the compassion in his eyes and drifted back to sleep.

When he woke again, Annie sat reading on Andre's cot. She smiled at him when he tried to sit up. "How do you feel?"

"Like crap." His voice cracked as he spoke. He looked around the tent. "Where is everyone?"

"Getting packed. The station radioed. We can leave this morning. We'll strike camp as soon as you're able to move around."

Max closed his eyes and exhaled in relief. His head hurt, body ached, and his skin itched. If he was going to be sick, he'd damn well rather do it in his own bed and not out on the ice.

His sweat smelled rank. He could only imagine what his breath was like. "I should get cleaned up."

Annie shifted. She focused on her lap. "Mac—"

"I'll be fine. It's the flu." He stood. She looked up at him, her eyes dark with worry. "Nothing a couple days in bed won't cure."

Max found a pot of tepid water left from breakfast. His hands shook as he dipped a cloth into the pot. He could feel Annie watching him. When he dipped it again, he hit the edge of the pan, and water splashed onto the floor. Cursing, Max bent to clean up. Fucking pan, fucking place, fucking goddamned world.

* * *

Andre stepped close to Max as they loaded the giant pile of gear into the snowcat. "I know you didn't intend to stop drinking. But that doesn't mean you have to start again. If you can hold on, it will get better. Promise. I'll help."

Max ground his teeth. He was getting tired of this One-Note Johnny. "What makes you think you know anything about my life?"

Andre leaned in, his lips almost brushing Max's ear. "How do you think I know about detox? You think you're this lone wolf whose problems no one can understand. You're not. I would not even need to be paying attention to know what's happening to you right now. Take this chance. If you don't, it will only get worse."

"Fuck you." Max hefted a crate into the back of the snowcat.

Andre's smile was sad. "Let me know when you're ready to accept help."

Max glared at him and stomped toward where Annie and Henrick were rolling up tents. The sooner they got packed up, the sooner he could get back to bed. And maybe his head would stop exploding and he could get some sleep.

* * *

One look at Max's face and Chief Jackson sent him directly to quarters. "I don't want to see you until you're well. And don't go spreading whatever shit you've got to the whole station."

So Max stumbled off, leaving Annie, Henrick, and Andre to unload. He slung his duffel into the room with a groan and sank onto the bed beside it. He stared at the row of liquor bottles he'd arrayed on top of the dresser at the foot of the bed. They called to him like the old friends they were. Stop drinking? Not when a drink was just what the doctor ordered. He had a cold. That was all. And his mother's cure for a cold had been four fingers of bourbon. Of course, that was his mother's cure for most things.

Max snagged a bottle of whiskey and held it to the light, rolling it back and forth. A tiny amber sun bounced through the liquid in rhythm with the shaking of his hand. Need pulsed through his body and he allowed himself a single moment of honesty. Andre was right. He didn't have the flu. And the only thing he could take to stop the goddamned headache felt smooth and cool in his hand. He balanced the bottle on his stomach. A straightforward, manly black-and-white label. Sour mash Kentucky straight bourbon whiskey since 1783. Max broke the seal. He held the bottle to his nose, inhaling until his nostrils stung. Bringing it to his lips, he took a long, hard pull. The bourbon burned his throat, and he sat, coughing. It felt like shafts of light flowing through his veins. He took another slug, and his headache started to fade.

Part Two

Mainbody

"One of the three seasons of the Antarctic year. At McMurdo, it starts around 1-October and goes until the last flight at Station Close, typically late February or early March."

—Dictionary of Antarctic Slang, Ethan Dicks

http://penguincentral.com/MCMslang.html

"Plane after plane arrives (weather permitting), disgorging hundreds of people and tons of cargo. The population triples, quadruples, quintuples in a matter of days. McMurdo becomes an incredible hive of activity. People work 60, 80, even 100 hour weeks. It's exciting, but it's nuts."

—Antarctica Online, "Life in Antarctica"

http://www.antarcticaonline.com/culture/culture.htm

Chapter Nine

"God, I hate summer." Annie craned her neck to see around the tall man in front of her in the lunch line. "All these people give me hives."

Max grinned. "You wouldn't have a winter job if it wasn't for all these people. Remember, we live to serve the scientific community."

"Fuck the scientific community." She tilted her head up and smiled sweetly at Max. "Ah, but that's what you'd like to do, isn't it?"

Max's heartbeat raced. He glanced around to see if anyone had heard. "Christ, Annie."

"Ah, sweetie, relax. I'm not worried that you'll leave me for another woman." Her grin widened, and she winked.

Across the dining hall, Max watched Andre's long back. Andre had been avoiding him for weeks, ever since Max signed Henrick's log, okaying him to dive. Max's relief at the lack of daily contact was tempered by an almost physical sense of absence. The man was terrifying—he could ruin Max's life.

And yet, the thought of that kiss kept him up way too many nights.

"You can't have it both ways," Annie had told him the night before as he poured out his confusion to her, his confession lubricated by several martinis sipped from a coffee mug.

Max had shaken his head. "Doesn't matter. The guy's got this thing against me anyway, thinks I'm a drunk."

"You are a drunk." She'd smiled and patted his knee. "And for a brave guy, you're a terrible coward. But I love you anyway."

Now, as the lunch line inched forward, Max wondered if she was right on both counts.

* * *

One of the things that had surprised Max his first summer on the ice was how fucking hot it was inside the dorms. He'd expected to spend long summer evenings bundled in thermals and fleece, and instead found himself in shorts and tees whenever he wasn't diving or working outside. They all did. Smitty favored gaudy Hawaiian shirts, and Bones tended toward T-shirts with sexually suggestive slogans. DIVERS DO IT DEEPER being one of his faves. Even Annie wore baggy tank tops under her even baggier overalls. Henrick walked around station wearing food-stained shorts, a pocket-rich safari vest, and shin-high black socks inside leather sandals. It annoyed even Max's ill-formed fashion sense.

In the context of the general McMurdo slovenliness, Andre always looked put together in freshly laundered tees and pressed jeans. Somehow, in his thirty-five-pound personal gear allotment, he must have found room for an iron. And he managed to pull off the whole over-groomed look. Where someone else might have come across as fussy, Professor Andre Dubois looked clean and professional. The other scientists and the contracted support staff all treated him with respect.

Whenever they were in the same room, Max watched Andre. He didn't want to think about why he was fascinated by the way Andre's hands moved when he spoke, the shape of his smile, or the way his hair grazed the back of his collar. Max found himself walking past the lab building or lingering in the dorm lounge, looking for Andre while pretending to himself that it was an accident whenever he spotted the tall, thin form. The guy had a quiet assurance that called to something deep in Max's gut. Too bad it would never work. Andre didn't drink and Max didn't fuck—not in Antarctica. Here at the bottom of the planet, all he did was dream. And he dreamed about Andre. A lot.

And then, one day, Andre disappeared out onto the ice, presumably sampling the ocean floor with Henrick and the others in his crew, and Max quit looking at anyone as he moved around the crowded, empty-feeling station.

* * *

Max stepped out of Gallagher's Pub and squinted against the glare of midnight sun off metal roofs. He leaned against the railing, inhaling the fresh scent of diesel and listening to the grind of a motor somewhere in the distance. He'd been shooting pool with Bones for shots, mostly winning, since Bones couldn't shoot for shit. Still, he'd had enough to be feeling fine. Saturday night was all right.

He headed toward the dorms, coat unzipped in the relative warmth of the twenty-degree night. The station looked as grubby as usual, but Max felt his heart expanding. He'd spent the week at the practice dive hut, checking out divers from all over the world—researchers and technicians passing through McMurdo on their way to field sites across the continent. Tomorrow was his day off. Tonight was all his. The only thing missing was someone to spend it with. But that wasn't an option now, was it? Even if Max wanted to bend his no-sex-in-Antarctica rule, the only guy he'd be interested in was out on the ice sampling sediment. Max shrugged. Maybe he'd take a bottle up to the summit of Mount Erebus and see what he could see.

He must have been drunker than he thought, because it didn't make sense that when he rounded the next blind corner, he almost ran over the man he'd been thinking about. Max stepped out of the way, stumbled, and straightened. He was pretty sure it wasn't a hallucination. "Dr. Dubois, hello. I thought you were out on the ice."

Andre stared down at him a moment. "We have a crew arriving Monday. I volunteered to drive back and get them. Pick up some supplies, that sort of thing."

Max nodded, not sure what to say.

Andre's gaze drifted down to the muddy path. "I stopped by your room to see how you were doing. Annie told me I'd find you at the bar."

Max raised his eyebrows. "You were coming to see me?"

Andre nodded and scraped a toe in the McMurdo muck. "I owe you an apology. I've thought about it a lot, and I think I've been unfair."

Max shifted his weight onto his other foot. "You don't need to apologize. I let you down out there on the ice, got sick, and wasn't good for anything."

Andre shook his head. "No, I overstepped. It's your life."

The wind blew a swirl of snow against Max's legs. He found himself riveted by the smooth line of Andre's jaw and the bead of saliva caught on his lower lip. Through the fume-laden air he smelled something light, spicy. He stepped closer. "You smell good."

Andre looked away. When he met Max's gaze, his cheeks, already flushed from the cold, darkened. "This is a very bad idea."

Max's heart rate picked up. He leaned toward Andre and whispered, "What is?"

A peal of laughter erupted, loud and near. Max and Andre stepped abruptly apart as a man and woman careened around the corner, arm in arm.

"'Scuse us," the woman called, bouncing off Andre as she swung by.

"Gotta get her to bed." Her companion winked at Max as they passed. "She's got an itch needs scratching."

She giggled. "You're so bad."

They staggered away.

Andre shook his head and turned back toward the dorms. "I'm sorry. I don't know what I was thinking."

Max grabbed his arm. "Where are you going?"

"To my room." Andre stood, shoulders slumped, facing away from Max.

Max tightened his grip and stepped closer. Fuck his rules. He could hardly hear himself speak for the pounding of his heart and the blood rushing to his crotch. "Mind if I come along?"

Andre stood very still, inhaled, exhaled, and slowly nodded. Max let go of his arm and fell in step beside him. The snow crunched beneath their feet. Their breaths puffed out in twin plumes. Neither man spoke as Andre led the way into the dorm, up the stairs, and down the hallway.

He stopped before a door covered in pictures of glaciers and cartoons from the *New Yorker*. He slid a key into the lock. "I share the room with Henrick. He stayed at camp." His hand on the knob, he turned to Max. "Don't pass out."

The room was dim after the glare of outside and the perpetual light of the hallway. Max kicked the door closed. His hands on either side of Andre's face, he pulled him into a long kiss. Andre's breath escaped in a rush. He sloughed off his coat, not breaking the kiss. Max let his own parka drop. Andre pushed him back against the door, hands locked on his hips, his tongue insistent, hungry.

Andre's face, freshly shaven, felt smooth beneath Max's hands. The scent of his aftershave rocketed through Max with a single message: this man wanted him. Tonight. Wanted him badly enough that he'd swallowed his pride, showered, shaved, and gone looking. Maybe only because Max was the only other queer on station, but it didn't matter. It had been a long time since he'd ended the night with a man who'd been looking specifically for him. It was fucking hot.

Max broke the kiss, pulling Andre's pristine shirt over his head and following it with his own more ragged tee. The muscles of Andre's back flexed beneath Max's hands, reminding him of the sleek play of seals. Andre leaned in. His thigh slipped between Max's. Andre felt hard and hot against Max's hip. His hands bracketed Max's head, holding him as he kissed deeply. Max pressed himself into the ridge of Andre's cock and slid his hands down to Andre's ass. Beneath the fabric of Andre's jeans, Max could feel muscles clenching, elongating as Andre rubbed against him. Andre's hand dived between them. He cupped Max through his jeans, his hand squeezing with each body thrust. Max moaned into his mouth, his fingers digging into the fabric covering Andre's ass.

Still kissing, Max launched them away from the door, walking Andre backward until they fell onto the narrow, neatly made bed. He scrambled with the zipper on Andre's jeans, hungry for the feel of him. Andre arched into his hand, lifting his hips and kicking out of his jeans. Max peeled down the tight European briefs. He wrapped his fingers around

Andre's hard length, smooth and hot. Max closed his eyes as he ran his hand up Andre's cock. Yes. He'd known there'd be this soft silk of a foreskin covering the tip. Max broke the kiss, wanting to see the long line of Andre's chest. As beautiful as he remembered. He let his gaze drop farther to the thick curls of Andre's pubic hair and the delicious sight of his straight, thick penis, the head sliding in and out of the foreskin with each stroke of Max's hand.

"You are incredibly fucking sexy," Max whispered as Andre thrust into his hand.

Andre sat up, rolling Max onto his back. In a few swift movements, he had Max naked. Andre licked his lips. "God help me, so are you."

Andre's mouth engulfed Max's, and they were skin to skin, and it felt magic, like diving under the ice, only warm like a hot spring. Max grasped Andre's bare ass, and the muscles rippled, alive beneath his fingers. Andre groaned and shifted until their cocks touched and slid together in exquisite friction. Max lost himself in the feel of Andre against him, the sound of their breath, the taste of his mouth, the smell of sweat and aftershave.

Andre pulled back, his eyes locked with Max's. "Here I come."

Max felt the pulsing of Andre's cock and watched the dilation of his pupils as he held Max's gaze. He closed his eyes and tumbled after, pulling Andre against him as he shot into their pressed flesh.

Max breathed in the warmth of Andre's weight. As their hearts slowed, he felt the race of Andre's pulse against his own. Max's head swam a little, and he smiled, relaxing into what was left of his buzz.

Andre rolled off him and stood. He picked up his shirt from the floor, wiped his belly, and tossed it to Max. "Sorry, there's no sink in the room. This will have to do."

Max leaned back on the bed, drinking in the sight of Andre naked. His legs were thicker, stronger than Max had imagined, and dark hair curled intriguingly down the insides of his thighs. He lifted his gaze to take in Andre's torso, the long ropes of his biceps.

Andre gestured toward the dorm-sized refrigerator in one corner of the room. "My hospitality is limited, but I have sparkling water if you'd like."

"Don't the French all drink wine?" Max sat up and ran a finger up the line of dark hair on Andre's belly.

Andre shivered. His hands settled on Max's shoulders. "There are a few of us who don't."

Max kissed Andre's salty-sweet belly. He felt relaxed and sexy, with enough of a buzz left to allow himself to let go.

Max ran his tongue along the groove of Andre's hip bone. Andre sighed. His hands brushed through Max's hair. "This is such a bad idea."

Max looked up, resting his chin against Andre's belly. "You keep saying that, but I don't think you mean it."

He laughed. "Oh, I mean it. It's just that I don't seem able to stop myself."

Max ran his hands from Andre's ass up his back and pulled him down on top of him. "I thought I was the one with a problem having sex in Antarctica. Isn't this what you wanted from me that night in the hotel?"

Andre rolled onto his side, facing him. He trailed a finger along Max's jaw. "Yes. And it wasn't a wise move then. But I was alone in a strange city and feeling sorry for myself."

"And tonight you got horny and needed to get laid." Max squeezed Andre's ass cheek. "That's normal enough."

He nodded, his gaze on Max's lower lip. "Even so, I knew you would taste like whiskey, and I've been clean a long time. You're not good for my sobriety, and I'm probably not good for yours."

Max snorted. "I'm not in the market for sobriety."

"I know." Andre rocked onto his back. "And there is the question of your comfortable closet."

"You're not going to go all preachy on me, are you?"

Andre shook his head, and Max kissed him. Andre slowly opened to him, and Max pressed in, his tongue making lazy, sexy circles in Andre's mouth. Max pulled back and whispered, "We're already here. We might as well make it a night. I'll leave before anyone's awake."

Andre bit his lower lip and looked into Max's eyes for a long time. Finally he gave a small nod and pulled Max into another soul-searing kiss. Heat roared in Max's veins. He threw himself on top of Andre, kissing him into the mattress. His knees straddled Andre's torso. His balls fell across Andre's stiffening cock. Andre held his face, his tongue danced in Max's mouth, tasting of kisses, inviting Max to dive deeper, kiss harder.

It was too much. It was not enough. Max slid his tongue out of Andre's mouth, across the smoothly shaved skin of his jaw, and down to his neck. He wanted to leave a mark, a bruise, something to let him know it wasn't a dream. Andre rolled his shoulder, and Max found himself sucking low on the collarbone, some sober part of his brain giving permission to brand this man there where no one else would see. Max let his teeth press into Andre's flesh, and Andre moaned, raking his fingernails down Max's back.

Max moved down Andre's chest, finding one nipple with his tongue and teasing the other with his fingers. Andre writhed beneath him, his cock pressing hard and hot into Max's gut. Max slid his thigh between Andre's, letting his own cock slide along Andre's balls. Max released the nipple, running his hand down Andre's smooth flesh to cup his ass.

Andre groaned something—it might have been French—and wrapped his leg around Max. Max ground his thigh into the crease of Andre's ass, pulling back to watch him arch. His breath caught as he saw Andre's face, skin flushed, mouth open, those gorgeous blue eyes lidded.

Max caught Andre's cock in his fist and growled, "I need to suck you or fuck you."

Andre's eyes opened, and his cock pulsed in Max's hand. He nodded toward the bedside table. "Condoms and lube in the top drawer. I'll get them."

Max rolled onto his back, releasing Andre and watching the way his muscles moved beneath his skin as he reached into the drawer. Max's buzz was fading, leaving behind a dull pain above his right eye. It didn't matter. Nothing mattered but the sight of Andre unwrapping a condom, the haunted look in his eyes as they met Max's, and the cool feel of latex as Andre unrolled the condom and dribbled lube onto Max's cock.

Andre held the base of Max's cock and leaned down to shove his tongue into Max's mouth for one short, hot kiss before sliding onto his side, his back to Max, his knees bent invitingly. Max rolled toward Andre, who held Max's cock and painted circles with it against the pucker of his ass. Max's mouth went to Andre's shoulder. Andre gasped and pushed back hard with his ass, taking in Max's cock in one long, even press. Max grabbed Andre's hip, holding them together while he felt Andre relax around him.

He wanted to fuck him slow, wanted to make it last all night, but Jesus, he felt good, tight, and hot. Max inhaled the smell of Andre's aftershave, now mixed with the scent of sex. He spit on his hand, reached around and clasped Andre's cock. Andre turned his head, and their mouths met in a sloppy, jolting kiss as Max began to move, thrusting in deep and fast, pumping Andre's cock with the same rhythm, pounding together into the night, diving deep and surfacing again and again, the clench of Andre's ass pulsing around Max's cock in rolling waves until they were both gasping and coming hard.

Later, as they lay side by side, their heartbeats returned to normal. Max ran a finger over Andre's biceps. "I'd forgotten your tattoo. I remember seeing it that morning in the hotel. Didn't think anything about it at the time, but barbed wire isn't the usual thing for a science guy."

Andre glanced at his arm, encircled by three loops of inky barbed wire. "I got it as a kid. I thought it looked tough. Now it reminds me of all the ways we imprison ourselves."

Max stroked the dark barbs. "'Clean a long time.' Does that mean you used to get out of control drunk?" He shook his head. "Sorry, can't picture it."

Andre lay on his back, staring at the ceiling. "Actually, alcohol was not my drug of choice. Too slow. I am more of a heroin guy."

That was a surprise. "You're joking."

Andre held the crook of his arm in front of Max's eyes. "Probably you can't see the scars in this light, but they're there. A few little dark spots that remind me of my youth."

Max held Andre's arm and peered at the pale flesh. If he squinted, he could almost imagine a constellation of dots. He let go, and Andre dropped his arm. Max frowned at him. "But you're a scientist. A PhD, right?"

Andre shrugged. "I haven't used since I was a teenager. But I could be on the streets again tomorrow." He rolled toward Max. "Maybe this time as a drunk. That's much more grown-up, yes?"

Max shook his head. "Sorry. I don't know grown-ups, just divers. We're not allowed to grow up."

"Will Annie be worried about you?" Andre caressed Max's shoulder. His hand felt warm, gentle.

Max leaned into the touch. It had been a long time since anyone stroked him like that. "She'll be fine. Either she'll assume I'm passed out on Smitty's floor, or she'll somehow get that I'm here."

"She knows?"

He inhaled the sweet smell of sex and kissed Andre's shoulder. "Annie knows everything about everyone. Not much gets by that girl. After the fire that killed her parents, she got shuffled between foster homes. Doesn't talk much, but what I've heard makes me understand why she's down here in Antarctica."

Andre smiled. "It's a funny place. You think you're going to spend all your time alone, but instead you're always surrounded by people."

Max smiled. "Not Annie. She's got that shop organized so that all she ever sees are mechanical objects in need of repair."

"Even out at camp there's no time alone. And it will get worse with the crew that comes in tomorrow. Another researcher and three graduate students." He stroked Max's jaw. "Will you be doing their Happy Camper training?"

Max tipped his head, and Andre's hand slid down his neck. "Not during mainbody. There's a safety crew in charge of that now." Max cleared his throat. "This new researcher. Is he someone you're close to?"

Andre's hand drifted along his shoulder and down his arm. "Yes, we're quite good friends. *She* brought me onto the project."

Max smiled, unreasonably happy at the pronoun. Which was crazy because it wasn't like this was going to be a long-term thing. Like Andre said, it was a bad idea. Still, nice to know competition wasn't on its way.

Andre's hand slid along Max's hip, sending a shiver of heat through him. "Annie calls you by your initials, M.A.C. What does the A stand for?" His fingers tickled as they brushed Max's belly.

"Alistair." Max arched into Andre's hand. He felt like a cat being petted.

Andre's hand stopped. "Maxwell Alistair. That's quite a name."

Max met his gaze. Andre's eyes crinkled at the edges.

"Maximilien." At Andre's raised eyebrows, he added, "My mom was into Regency romance novels. I have a brother named Phineas who's a cop in Chicago. His middle name is Fredrick. Last I saw him, he was going by Fred."

Andre's laugh was deep and warm. "Your mother sounds like a character."

Max shook his head to clear it. Talking about his mother was always a buzzkill. "She had her moments."

Max closed his eyes, seeing again his beautiful mother lying in bed, pills and scotch spilled on the floor beside her. He tried to hold on to his rapidly fading buzz, but he was getting disturbingly sober. He needed to start carrying a hip flask.

* * *

Max's watch said three a.m. Time to go. He looked down at Andre dozing beside him. Andre looked beatific with his dark curls cascading across his cheek, the bruise from Max's kiss blooming on pale skin along the ridge of his collarbone. Max wanted to brush back the curls, to once again run his fingers through their silky softness. He was acutely aware of the summer stretched out before them. Distance and secrecy would combine, and they were unlikely to have another night like this.

He wasn't sure how he felt about Andre, but Jesus, the sex had been great.

Max slid from bed, careful not to disturb him. He fumbled across the floor for his clothing. He could write a note, but what would it say? He slipped into clothes, quietly opened the door, and let himself out into the hallway. Blinking in the light of the corridor, he shrugged into his parka and prepared for the short, cold walk through the bright night to his own dorm.

Chapter Ten

The next morning, Andre wasn't at breakfast. At lunch, Max saw him surrounded by a group of strangers wearing the spotless pants and boots of new recruits. Andre caught Max's eye for a moment. He touched the spot on his collarbone where Max had kissed him the night before. Max swallowed hard. Someone laughed, and Andre turned back to focus on his own group. The message seemed clear. The night had been amazing, but now it was time to move on. Max slumped over his chili dog.

"What's with you?" Bones asked through a mouthful of food. "You look like someone ran over your grandmother."

"Does Max have a grandmother?" Smitty asked, shoveling his way through a second dessert. "I can't imagine him sitting down with Granny to a plateful of cookies, can you?"

"That the new batch going out to the dive camp?" Bones nodded toward the cluster around Andre. "A couple sweet-looking girls in there. I wouldn't mind getting a chance to know them better."

"You are the worst pussy hound I know." Smitty slugged his arm, his own eyes fixed on the group. "Still, someone's gotta do their checkout dives."

Max rolled his eyes at them both. "Can't you guys think of anything but sex?"

Smitty and Bones looked at each other.

"No," they said in unison and burst out laughing.

Max watched the group fluttering around Andre. He had a sudden, visceral memory of Andre kissing him, his tongue pressing deep into Max's mouth. Max could almost feel the rough scratch of Andre's teeth against his tongue, and it sent a shiver down his spine. Max closed his eyes and took a deep breath. He could use a drink.

When he opened them, he smiled. "Hey, guys, it's our day off. Let's hit Gallagher's."

* * *

If the new dive crew passed through Gallagher's later that evening, Max didn't know it. After doing boilermakers in Smitty and Bones's room, he passed out on their rug and woke with the acrid smell of vomit caught in his nose. He opened his eyes and looked at the floor where he'd been sleeping. Nope, wasn't his. Raising his pounding head a few inches from the floor, he spied Smitty rinsing out his shoe. Max groaned and let his head fall back to the floor.

Bones kicked his leg. "We missed breakfast. If we're not in the chief's office in ten minutes, he'll have our hides."

Max eased into a seated position as his stomach clenched. He closed his eyes, but the room started spinning. He flicked them back open. "You got any aspirin?"

Smitty tossed him a bottle. Max shook four pills into his palm, dry swallowed, and slowly stood. His mouth felt like a desert. His head hurt every time he moved. Not good for a workday.

"I gotta get some coffee," he muttered, stumbling into his shoes.

Smitty growled, "Chief'll have some going. Let's move."

Chief Jackson wrinkled his nose as the three men entered his office. "You smell like a distillery. What were you three monkeys up to last night?"

Max looked at his shoes. "Sorry, Chief. It kind of got away from us."

Chief Jackson shook his head. "It's like working with kindergartners. You'd better get down to the dive locker. There are a dozen new divers to outfit and check out."

Max looked longingly at the full coffeepot.

Chief Jackson sighed. "All right, go ahead. But drink up. I don't want them waiting all morning for you."

"Yes, sir." Max poured a full cup of coffee and brought it to his lips, letting the scorching liquid burn his tongue. His mouth and throat throbbed when he finished, but at least his head began to clear.

Chief Jackson snorted. "SEALs. Fucking inhuman."

* * *

Max was standing in the dive locker sorting equipment when Andre brought his new crew members in. Max's and Andre's eyes met. Andre's gorgeous blues looked into Max's undoubtedly bloodshot browns.

Andre's voice was soft. "Are you okay to dive?"

Max nodded. "I'm fine."

Andre searched his face for a long time. "Be careful. Don't do anything you'll live to regret."

"I said I was fine." Max looked away, focusing on the rack of thermals and the dank smell of rubber and fleece.

"You don't look it. Try not to kill my crew." Andre touched Max's arm. "Or yourself." Before Max could respond, Andre stepped away and began pulling young divers into the room. "Line up so that Mr. Conway can outfit you with your suits."

"It's just Max," he grumbled, turning to the first in line. "What are you, a large?"

* * *

Everyone checked out this time, and two days later, they left for the ice. Not that Max saw Andre in the meantime, except across the room at meals. Still, the first evening after he'd watched the big red van pull away from the station, even though he stood in line for half an hour and nearly every seat was taken, the dining hall felt to Max like an empty room.

He needed a drink. Max settled into his seat beside Bones, across from Smitty, and sighed. The smell of overcooked vegetables and boiled meat made his stomach roll. He took his tray to the dishwashers and walked outside. Another beautiful evening in McMurdo, where engines roared, the scent of diesel filled the air, and the only birdsong came from skuas dive-bombing residents and garbage piles for food. What the fuck made him decide to make a living down here? He trudged back to his room and a half-empty bottle of scotch.

* * *

Max added another juice to his tray, his head pounding as he navigated through the light and clatter of breakfast. He collapsed into a seat next to Bones.

Bones looked up from his eggs. "You look like shit, man."

Max downed an orange juice. He closed his eyes as the world tilted with his head.

Smitty gestured at Max with his fork. "When I left you at the bar last night, you were already fucked-up. What happened with that chick from the machine shop you were chatting up? I hope you kept it in your pants. Annie'd have your hide."

Max squinted at Smitty. "Who?"

Smitty laughed. "The big one. Short hair, looks like a dyke. Man, you were doing shots together all night. Don't you remember?"

Max scanned his memory of the night before, which was mostly a black hole. It took a while before the image of Marge—could that really be her name?—drifted up out of the mist. She'd been telling him about a breakup with her girlfriend. Beyond that, he couldn't remember. He hoped to hell he'd kept his mouth shut.

Chief Jackson appeared beside the table. "Morning, boys." He peered down at Max. "What, was it Tequila Tuesday and no one told me?"

Max shrugged. He couldn't find a witty comeback.

Chief Jackson looked at him for a long time. "Smith and Bonair are on dive duty today. You look like a candidate for dead diver syndrome. I'm putting you in the equipment room. There are a couple regulators that need repair."

Max pushed a pile of eggs around his plate and nodded.

Jackson's voice went soft. "Stop by my office first. We need to talk."

Max could feel Smitty and Bones exchanging glances as the chief walked away. Fuck them all. He didn't feel like diving anyway.

* * *

Chief Jackson was standing by the coffee machine as Max walked in. The chief waved him toward the chair in front of his desk, poured two cups, and handed him one.

Max nodded his thanks. "You wanted to see me?"

Jackson sat in his chair and stared at Max over his cup. Steam billowed from the mug as he blew on it. "Something you want to talk with me about, son?"

Max shook his head, regretting the movement as pain shot through his frontal lobe. "No, sir. Not that I can think of, sir."

Jackson nodded and sipped his coffee. "The reason I ask is that this is the third time in a week I've had to take you off dive duty."

Max felt that peculiar churn of self-pity, humiliation, and nausea that sometimes came with a hangover. He stared into his coffee cup. "I'm sorry, sir."

Jackson set his cup on the desk and leaned toward Max. "Damn it, you're my best diver. I depend on you. I know you guys have to blow off steam every now and then. I've been in the Navy my whole life, for Christ's sake. But you're pushing my limits."

Max closed his eyes. His head pounded, and his body ached. Disgust welled in him like a stain. "Are you going to send me home, sir?"

Jackson sat back, crossing his arms over his chest as he looked at Max. "Not yet. But I'm warning you. This kind of behavior has to stop. I don't care what you do in your downtime, but it can't interfere with your job."

Max focused on a spot in the middle of Chief Jackson's desk. "Yes, sir. I understand."

"Good. Now get out of here." Jackson waved his hand dismissively.

Max stood, placed the still full coffee mug on his desk, and walked as purposely as he could toward the door and down the corridor to the equipment repair room. Once there, he slumped against the wall and closed his eyes, letting the humiliation roll through him. At least Andre wasn't on station to see this.

* * *

Outside of the meteorologists, Annie was probably the only one paying attention to the summer solstice. Somehow the longest day of the year lost its meaning when the sun didn't set for months. But for Annie the day had spiritual implications.

After dinner, Smitty suggested Gallagher's. Bones was in the mood for the other bar, Southern Exposure. Max declined both and headed back to the room. As he opened the door, the woody scent of patchouli incense bit into his nostrils. It was like walking into a head shop. The blackout curtains were drawn, and Annie floated around the room, dressed in white and lighting the candles she'd balanced on every available surface. He would have felt irritated, but she smiled her half smile at him, and he softened. If she wanted to be queen of the gypsies, that was her business.

He grabbed his paperback—a tattered crime story he'd found at the bottom of a bin Chief Jackson had him clean out—and stretched out on his bunk, ignoring the sexy call of the almost full tequila bottle sitting on the bedside table. Eventually Annie swallowed the tab and cocooned herself into her bunk. The candles burned on. Max tried to follow the plot of the book and keep the characters straight. All he knew was that people kept getting shot, and his mind filled with the crack of guns. He could almost smell sulfur, blood, and dust on the road after some fanatic decided to blow up a transport. Max threw down the book and sat, his muscles twitching with restlessness. His gaze fell on a basket of unfolded laundry. That was something he could do.

He folded a T-shirt and dropped it back on top of the rest. He picked at a clod of dirt stuck in the treads of his boot. Standing, he paced to the window and peeked out through the curtains. Sun glinted off machinery, the road outside the window a mix of black volcanic dirt and filthy snow. In the distance, Mount Erebus rose above it all. Max wondered what Andre was doing in his camp out on the ice. It seemed far away, their night together a long time ago. He let the blind fall back into place. He leaned against the wall and looked at Annie. She smiled at him.

"Is it good?" he whispered.

Her smile widened. "Beautiful."

He nodded and paced back to his bed. As he picked up the novel, his fingers brushed the bottle of tequila he'd been working hard to ignore. He stared at the piss-yellow liquid. He glanced at Annie, smiling softly on her bunk. Maybe one shot wouldn't hurt. Something to take the edge off his mood.

* * *

Someone was shaking him. Max opened an eye to see Andre looming over him. Max grinned. "Hey, what are you doing here?"

Andre's expression was stern. "Get up. It's Annie."

"Annie?" Max struggled to sit, trying to clear his head and blinking away the pain behind his eyes. Annie. He'd been babysitting Annie. "What happened— Shit. Is she okay?"

Andre pulled him out of bed. "Come see for yourself."

Max blinked into the bright hallway lighting and tried to keep up as Andre trotted down the corridor. He shook his head, but the half-drunk fuzziness persisted. He could hear shouting but couldn't make out the words.

As they turned the corner into the dorm lounge, he heard Annie shout, "Get away from me, you motherfucker." There was a crack, a curse, and the crowd parted. Max saw Annie, still in her white gown, holding a wrench over Bones, who knelt in front of her, gingerly touching his bleeding temple.

Max grabbed him by the collar and pulled him up. "What did you do to her?"

"Nothing." Bones shook his head. "I was trying to get her to calm down."

Max became aware of Andre's hand on his shoulder. "No one can convince her to go back to the room. You need to try."

Max dropped Bones and turned to Annie. She was looking at him with a wild-eyed wariness. She didn't seem to recognize him. He squeezed his eyes shut, trying to clear his head.

"Somebody stop her," a voice said, and Max's eyes flew open. He saw Annie heading for the door. He stared after her for a moment too long. She hauled the door open and ran out into the bright sunlight, wearing a flimsy nightgown. Barefoot.

The crowd surged after her, and by the time he could get to the doorway, he had to push through a knot of people standing in the foyer watching Annie running through the frozen McMurdo mud.

"She has ten minutes to frostbite." Max was vaguely aware of Andre speaking from the corner, where he was pulling on boots.

Max took a deep breath. *If you don't mind, it don't matter.* He ran out the door and after Annie. The first touch of his bare foot on ice sent a spike of pain up his leg. The wind cut into the bare skin of his arms. His heart pounded as he sucked in lungfuls of icy air. Annie was fast. Max pushed himself to run faster, to ignore the pain in his feet and his lungs. With her gown billowing in the wind, she looked like a cover model for one of his mother's romance novels, an eighteenth-century distressed virgin.

She must have heard him behind her because suddenly she stopped and spun around, her wrench held high. Max ducked and slammed into her, knocking away the wrench and scooping her up and over his shoulder. He ran back toward the dorm, Annie pounding on his back.

The medics met him halfway. They grabbed Annie, bundled her in blankets, and carried her off. Max stood watching them, oblivious to the pain in his feet and the sting of the wind against his skin.

Someone was wrapping a blanket around his shoulders and prodding him the last few steps to the dorm. "Come on, *mon ami*. You'll hurt yourself."

Max let Andre guide him through the chattering throng to the lounge.

Someone had filled a pan with warm water. Max was pushed into a chair, and his feet were thrust in. Within seconds, the numbness disappeared, replaced by excruciating bolts of pain as blood returned to wake up the nerve endings.

People babbled around him. At the moment, they saw him as a hero. That would change once they figured out that none of it would have happened if he'd stayed awake in the first place. And even if they never knew that, Annie would. It was the one thing she'd made him promise—not to drink when she dropped.

Andre put a hand on his shoulder. "Do you think you can walk now? Maybe you should get those feet checked."

Max shook his head and stood. "I'll be fine." He took a step. It felt like walking on nails. He gritted his teeth against the pain and took another step. *If you don't mind, it don't matter.*

"I'll walk you back to your room, to be sure." Andre's tone was firm. Max shrugged and pushed his way through the crowd.

He tried not to limp down the corridor. The rough nub of the carpet seemed to cut into his feet.

Andre didn't speak until he'd closed the door to Max and Annie's room. He turned to Max, his face concerned. "What's she on?"

Max sank onto his bunk. The candles had burned out, and the patchouli smelled cheap and old in the harsh fluorescent light. "Acid."

Andre fingered the tapestry cocooning Annie's bed. "That explains the hand-waving. At least they can't test for that."

Max watched him move around the room. "What happened?"

Andre looked down at him. "I'm sure we'll learn more at breakfast. Gossip is a hobby here. What I know is that she came into the lounge, where I was having coffee with my colleagues, looking and talking like Shakespeare's Ophelia— white gown, incoherent speech, and all that."

Max slumped forward, head in hands. "Who all saw her?"

Andre shrugged. "Does it matter? You saw the people who were there tonight, but by noon tomorrow everyone will know. And your friend Mr. Bonair may have quite the wound to add spice to the story."

Max groaned. "Annie doesn't like to be touched. Not by strangers."

"He was trying to get her to come back to the room when I came to get you. Apparently she doesn't like him. It looked like that's when the trip turned for her." He gestured toward the last sputtering candle. "She was having a good time until then."

"It's my fault." Max hit his forehead with the heel of his hand. "I was supposed to keep watch, but I fell asleep."

Andre picked up the empty tequila bottle. "Fell asleep?"

Max grimaced.

"So she asked you to take care of her while she tripped?" Andre picked a piece of lint from his pants.

Max threw himself back on the bed, his arm over his eyes. "That's been our deal for years."

Andre dropped the bottle into the recycling bin and dusted off his hands. He touched Max's shoulder gently. "We need to clean this room of drugs. The security guards, they will be here in the morning to search."

Max stared at him. "I can't dump Annie's LSD. She'll kill me."

"Ah, *mon cochon*, will it not be worse if you both are deported to jail?" He patted Max's shoulder. "Come on. Time to flush."

Max fumbled through Annie's drawer until he found her special box. He held it out to Andre.

* * *

Max watched the shredded paper swirl in the toilet. He turned to Andre. "Why are you at the station?"

Andre leaned in the open doorway watching, arms crossed. "I arrived this afternoon. We need a real lab to finish processing our samples. The crew voted to time it so that we'll be here through New Year's. Mostly, I believe, because there's a rumor the food will be good. Besides, a few new workers are arriving on the first flight in after Christmas."

Max ran water in the sink and splashed his face. "I really fucked up this time."

Andre's eyes were hooded as he gazed at Max. "Yes, you did."

Max pulled a paper towel from the dispenser. "Annie's tough, though. She'll be all right."

Andre shrugged. "Maybe so, but she'll be angry with you."

"Fuck." Max pushed past him and trudged toward the room.

Andre followed. He rested a hand on Max's back. "Take care of her. And remember that this too shall pass."

Max paused with his hand on the doorknob. "Staying sober when she got high was the only thing she ever asked me to do."

"Do you want me to stay?" Andre's hand was comforting on his shoulder. But the only thing Max wanted was to curl up with a bottle and make the whole evening go away.

He shook his head. "I'm not good company tonight. Thanks, though."

Andre nodded. With a last pat on Max's shoulder, he strode down the corridor. Max opened the door and entered his room.

* * *

Max looked at Annie huddled on an infirmity bed, a blanket wrapped around her shoulders. The room felt hot, but Annie shivered. The bright white room smelled of disinfectant, and Annie looked pathetic. The filthy hem of her white dress poked from beneath the blanket. Thick white bandages covered her feet.

Her eyes were cold and dark as she looked at him. "Prick."

Max winced. "I'm sorry."

She shook her head and looked away.

The doctor appeared, looking very McMurdo in jeans and tee. "Hey, Max. How are you? I heard you sprinted out into the snow too. You want me to take a look at your feet?"

Max shook his head. "I'm fine. How's Annie?"

"Still in the room." She glared at him. "And it's none of your business, asshole."

The doctor blushed. "We tested her for drugs. Didn't find anything. I'm writing this up as an allergic reaction. But you might want to take better care of her next time.

Annie snorted. "Like that's going to happen."

"Maybe you should leave now." The doctor shuffled Max into the hallway. Before closing the door on Max, he muttered, "If my girlfriend wanted to drop on station, I'd sure as hell keep an eye on her. But I guess to each his own."

Max stood staring at the closed door, wondering what was next.

* * *

"I don't want you here anymore." Annie hadn't left her bed all day. The tray of food Max had brought from the dining hall lay untouched on her bedside table.

Max ran a hand through his hair. "Look, I told you I'm sorry. When this all dies down, I'll get you more. I promise."

She scowled at him. "You don't get it, do you? It's not the acid. I can live without that. It's a tool. What I can't get over is how you abandoned me."

Max clenched his fists. "I fell asleep."

She shook her head. "No, you got drunk. Like every other night. Like you promised me you wouldn't do when I needed you." She turned her back on him. "I'll talk to the housing manager tomorrow, but in the meantime, please find somewhere else to stay."

Max stared at her, openmouthed and angry. He grabbed his coat and slammed out of the room. He stomped down the corridor, out the door, into the bright evening sun, and made his way across the station to Gallagher's. Fuck Annie. He didn't need her anyway.

Chapter Eleven

After a couple of nights on Bones and Smitty's floor, Max gulped back his pride and allowed the housing manager to allot him a bunk in a quad room. Room assignments at McMurdo were about comfort and status. With Annie, their status as old-timers bought them a double with a sink in the room next to a bathroom they only had to share with one other couple. Kicked out midseason, he was stuck in a sinkless room with three newbie guys, sharing a shower with half the building. Not to mention the disgusted looks he got.

"Way to go, asshole." This from the barber who changed girlfriends twice a season.

"Bastard," a woman in the food line served up with his mashed potatoes.

"You're a real prick, you know that," asked the bartender at Gallagher's as she ignored his request for another drink. If Smitty hadn't held him back, Max might have thrown his glass at her. Instead, he slapped it on the counter and marched out into the relentless sun.

On McMurdo, everyone knew everything. And everyone had an opinion. Maybe somewhere else the crowd would have turned on Annie for doing drugs. But here, the general consensus was that Max should have taken care of her. And he couldn't agree more. So for the most part, he let the condemnation roll through him, unwilling to fight back. Maybe he drank a little more, but who could blame him? It was Annie's continued silence that really hurt, the way her eyes skittered away from his face. It was the same look new people gave her. In some psychic way, his betrayal had disfigured him in her eyes and the eyes of those around them.

Only Bones and Smitty still talked with him at meals, their conversation uncharacteristically careful.

"She'll come around." Bones jostled Max with his shoulder.

Smitty nodded. "Annie's good people. She can't stay mad forever."

Max shrugged and pushed food around his plate.

The only other face that didn't register disgust was Andre's. The look he gave Max was more painful, a sad mix of pity and regret that pierced him every time he saw it.

Max started to avoid the dining hall, living on chips and candy purchased at the same little store that sold postcards and tees to residents and tourists alike.

Annie weathered the shitstorm with grace. She put the room back together after the security guards' search to accommodate her new roommate, a pale woman who researched penguins and needed a bed between stints on the ice. Max doubted anyone believed it, but since nothing illegal had been found in Annie's blood or the room, the doc's version held, and she had officially suffered some sort of allergic reaction. A less skilled mechanic without her ice time might have had more trouble, but it appeared Annie was as Teflon as it got at McMurdo.

* * *

The dive locker smelled of neoprene and wet clothes. Max was hiding out after hours, polishing off the last of Annie's gifted bottles when Andre appeared in the doorway. Outlined by the bright hallway light, he looked like his own shadow. Max stared at him blearily.

"Hey. Dive shop's closed." He gestured with the bottle. "Want some? Oh, yeah, that's right. You don't drink. And I'm not good for your sobriety." He tipped up the bottle and chugged. "Guess you're right. Not good for anything else."

Andre stepped in and sat on the bench beside him. "It's Christmas Eve."

Max nodded. "Yep. Holly jolly and all that."

Andre stretched out his long legs and leaned his back against a locker. "I came to see if you wanted to get some dinner. But it looks like that wouldn't be a good idea right now."

"Annie gave me this." Max held the bottle up to the light. "It's almost gone. I didn't want to share it with my new roommates, but I'd share it with you."

Andre shook his head. "Thank you. That's actually quite a sweet offer. But no. Go ahead and finish it yourself."

Max leaned forward, resting his forearms on his thighs. "It's not like I meant to—"

"Pass out?" Andre offered, his voice quiet in the silent room.

"Yeah, pass out. I would never abandon Annie. She's my best friend." He took another swig of whiskey. "I'm the one that's supposed to protect her."

"I know. Under all that machismo and intoxication you're a very good man." Andre rested a hand on Max's back. "Annie'll be okay. And she might even forgive you someday."

"Yeah, right." Max ran a hand through his short hair. "It better be soon. I don't think the chief's gonna invite me back next year. He hasn't put me out on a dive in weeks."

Andre's hand warmed Max's back. He stroked gently as he spoke. "Maybe you can turn it around."

Max shook his head. "Fuck it."

They sat in silence for a long time. Max stood, drained the last of the whiskey, and threw the bottle in the recycling bin. "Go have your Christmas dinner. I'm gonna head to Gallagher's and see if I can get that bitch of a bartender to serve me."

Tipping up his chin, Andre looked into his eyes. Max stared into those deep blue pools.

Andre smiled softly. "Let me know when you want to change direction. It really is better on the other side."

The kiss he planted on Max's forehead tingled for a long time.

* * *

Max's head hurt. His mouth felt full of sand. He stared at his coffee cup, reached into his back pocket, and brought out the flask he'd found hidden in the chief's bottom drawer. He added a dollop of brandy to his coffee. Only two days into the week, and he'd already drunk his allotted bottle of whiskey. Unless he could scam something soon, he'd be back begging to buy drinks from that bitch bartender at Gallagher's, where his money ought to be as good as anyone else's.

He tried to focus on the mound of paperwork in front of him. Fucking inventory sheets. What did the chief think he was, an office boy?

The locker room door opened, and Henrick strode in, wearing his characteristic sneer. "I need gear to train a new student on our sampling technique."

Max snorted. "Now you're doing checkout dives?"

Henrick straightened, peering down his nose at Max. "Your Mr. Smith will certify her diving, but Dr. Dubois has delegated the sampling exhibition to me."

Max sat back, rubbing his temples to ease the throb of his headache. "You talking about the tiny, redheaded chick with the sunburst tattoo? I got her outfitted yesterday."

Henrick crossed his arms over his chest. "I'm glad to hear that you're doing your job. However, all my equipment is back at camp."

Max shrugged and nodded toward the equipment room. "You know where everything is. Knock yourself out." He turned his attention to the paperwork, sipping spiked coffee and hoping the idiot wouldn't bang things around too loudly.

After he left, Max wandered into the equipment room. He glanced at the red shelf. Had he told Henrick to stay away from the bin of broken equipment? He shook his head. It was all labeled. Even Henrick wouldn't be that fucking dumb.

* * *

The winds quieted on New Year's Eve. The temperature hovered somewhere around freezing, and everyone walked around with their parkas unzipped, enjoying the warmth of midsummer Antarctica. All day people buzzed around, getting ready for Icestock—the annual music festival with which the station rung in the new year. Fragments of music erupted from the stage as the bands ran sound checks. Here and there figures appeared in half-formed costumes. Steam rising from big pots of simmering chili mixed with the usual smells of diesel and dirt. New Zealanders began to arrive from their base a few miles away. Max leaned against a tractor and tried to stay out of the way. He was out of booze, and no one would sell him any. He hadn't had a drink since the night before and was feeling like crap. All he could hope for was the event's free beer.

Smitty appeared. He handed Max a beer. "Better lay low for a while. Chief's looking for you, and it isn't pretty."

Max's hand shook as he cracked open the can and took a long, deep pull. The cheap beer tasted like piss water, but he guzzled half the can in one long slug. Something deep inside began to relax.

He focused on Smitty. "What's wrong now?"

Smitty scuffed his boot in the dirt, not looking at Max. He sipped his own beer. A guitar squealed from the stage. "Something about a missing flask."

Max grimaced. "Shit. Thanks for telling me."

Smitty tipped back his beer and considered the stage. "You hear about that fucking German?"

Max glanced at him. "Henrick? What now?"

Smitty shook his head. "Fucker was out at the practice hut trying to impress some girl and jumped in with a broken regulator."

Max stared at Smitty. "Broken? As in you can't breathe through it? Is he okay?"

Smitty nodded. "Yeah. Word is he panicked, and the chick had to go in after him. Says he's never diving again." Smitty watched the stage. "Christ knows where he got that busted regulator. Guess it had red marking tape on the hose, so he must have pulled it out of the repair bin. Fucking moron."

Max blinked. He knew exactly when and where Henrick had picked up the faulty regulator.

Smitty drained his bottle. "I gotta go get ready. Bones scored a sweet set of Viking helmets, found them in some old storage bin. But I thought you should know the chief's looking for you about his flask. Maybe now's not a good time to be hanging out in public."

Max stared after him as he crossed the yard and disappeared behind a building. Henrick had gone underwater with a broken regulator that he'd picked up when Max was too hungover to check. The thought hit Max hard. He had to hold on to the tractor to keep from falling down. Luck was all that had kept him from murder.

Some woman onstage kept saying, "Check. Check." And it felt like an accusation.

He looked at the half-empty beer in his hand. Setting it carefully on the ground, Max stumbled away from the Icestock clearing. Self-disgust boiled up so quickly that he stopped and bent over, sure he was going to vomit. The wave passed, and he trudged on, his only conscious destination *away*. As he walked, the events of the summer tumbled through his mind, beginning in the hotel when he passed out on Andre. From there it had only gotten worse, until big bad Max Conway was stumbling drunk on the job, so drunk the chief couldn't trust him. Shouldn't trust him. He'd let fucking Henrick leave with a dead-trap regulator. No one should trust him, not Andre or the chief, not even Annie. He'd abandoned her and nearly killed Henrick. The memories swirled through his brain, each carrying a unique flavor of shame.

By the time he reached the practice dive hut at the station's edge, he was panting. All those years of work and pride, and here he was, a pathetic shambles, not fit for human company. No wonder Annie hated him and Andre looked at him with pity. He pictured those kind, sad eyes and groaned. His self-image as a lone wolf cracked before the sudden understanding that he was nothing but a scared little boy. All his strongman stuff, his SEAL training, his combat experience… All they meant were he could take life. He was very good at that. Living himself? He sucked.

Max tripped over the threshold of the dive hut and fell, hitting his cheek against the floor. He curled into a fetal position, cradling his throbbing cheek. The waves of shame kept coming. It seemed like he'd been failing people all his life. Annie, the Brooklyn kid who died in Afghanistan by driving into an ambush Max should have seen, the men he'd fucked, whose numbers he'd purposely lost, his brother who didn't even know where he fucking was.

Max stared at the dark hole in the center of the hut. He crawled to the dive hole and knelt, looking into the dark water where Henrick had almost died a second time. If he slid through this ice window, maybe he'd fall into a deep blue sleep. He shuddered out an exhausted sigh. His father had always said Max was just like his mother. She'd surrendered. Maybe he should too. It would be easy. The cold would be shocking at first, but then he'd go numb. In BUD/S once, when his regulator was torn from his mouth, he'd inhaled a lungful of seawater. He'd made it to the surface and choked the water out, coughing for a long time, treading water, and praying for enough time to recover before an instructor attacked him again. He'd woken with nightmares of drowning for months afterward, still did whenever he got too sober. Death by drowning—wouldn't that be ironic? They said that once you passed through the panic of that first breath, after the fighting spirit of survival thrashed through your body, there was peace. Incredible, sweet, everlasting peace.

Max closed his eyes. What would it matter to anyone if he slipped into that cold darkness and never came back? Who would miss him? The image of Andre rose in his mind, like he was there before him, floating above the dive hole. Max remembered Andre's eyes, soft when he'd come to take Max to Christmas Eve dinner, sad as he gazed across the room when everyone else shunned Max, dark as Andre had held him when they moved together that one wonderful night. He heard Andre's soft voice, with that little hint of an accent, telling him he'd be there if Max wanted to turn it around.

He took one last look at the cold water. "Maybe another day," he whispered into the depths. He stood, swaying a little. Opening the flap of his jacket, he wiped his face with the hem of his sweatshirt. He probably looked like hell and smelled worse. He should hit the showers before going in search of Andre.

At the door of the hut, he stopped. A figure crossed the ice toward him with long-legged strides. Max rubbed his eyes. It was like one of those magic stories where thinking made it so. He watched, slack-jawed, as Andre neared.

He stopped a few feet from Max. "Someone said they saw you going this way. Smitty told me you were upset."

Max bit his lip. "Henrick…"

Andre shook his head. "I'm glad he's given up diving. That man should never go underwater."

Max's hands curled into fists. He pounded one against his chest. "It's my fault. I let him go out with broken gear. I was too fucked-up to notice what he was taking."

Andre's eyebrows arched. "I wondered if that might have been how he got the damaged gear." He touched Max's arm. "Take responsibility for the failed dive if you like, but Henrick should have checked his regulator before going under. Would you dive in without making sure you could breathe first?"

Max shook his head.

He stared at Andre for a long time. It felt like the moment right before combat began, when everything was very quiet and you knew it was all about to explode. "I can't go on like this. Can you help me?"

Andre's smile was brighter than the midnight sun. He pulled Max into his arms. "Oh, *mon chéri*, of course I'll help."

In the distance, a speaker crackled to life. "Welcome to Icestock. Let's rock in the new year!"

Chapter Twelve

Max sulked, huddled in his parka in the back of the vehicle. Around him, people chattered, laughed, and teased each other. Beside him, Andre discussed research with a blonde woman, one of a dozen people Max had been introduced to but whose names he couldn't be bothered to remember. Andre's thigh pressed against Max's with reassuring pressure.

The black cloud inside Max's head pulsed with the ebb and flow of sounds. He still wasn't sure he'd made the right choice the night before. He'd thrown himself into Andre's offer of assistance, but maybe the deep blue water would have been better. If he was dead, he wouldn't be bumping along, steeped in humiliation and self-pity, heading for the dive camp. Not to work as a diver, but as some sort of general grunt. Max closed his eyes. A deeper wave of shame rolled through him as he remembered how relieved Chief Jackson had been to see him go.

The old man's gruff voice rumbled through his memory. The chief hadn't looked at Max but had spoken instead to

Andre. "You're welcome to him. Drunk divers make dead divers."

The vehicle rolled to a stop. Max peered through the window. The camp had changed since his last stay. The dive hut remained, but two long portable buildings stood where the tents had been.

Andre touched his arm. "We're here. Come help unload."

Max trailed after him, feeling like a cross between a prisoner and a puppy. He could use a drink. But according to his deal with Andre, that wasn't going to happen. He pushed back panic. He'd been a SEAL. He could do anything. Mind over matter. Max kept breathing, kept walking, and did whatever he was told. Time had slowed to a crawl, and he was slogging through each minute.

As the last few bundles were hauled out of the vehicle, Andre handed a box to Max. "We'll take these down to the dive hut."

Max crossed the threshold of the hut and was hit by an avalanche of memory. He remembered feeling confident and brave. He'd owned this hut. And Andre had kissed him here, leaving him panting and wanting more.

Andre set his box in one corner. He gestured for Max to do the same.

As Max straightened, Andre caught his face between his hands. "I'm glad you're here."

Max snorted. "I don't know why. No one else is."

Andre's thumb caressed his jaw. "I don't think anyone else cares one way or the other. Although they're probably more than a little curious."

"What, they don't know you're Mr. Twelve-Step Antarctica?" Max tried to smile, but it must not have worked because Andre's brow furrowed.

"I can drive you back to the station if you like."

Max pulled away and walked toward the dive hole. "There's nothing to go back to, except an ugly dismissal and a plane to Christchurch."

Andre stayed silent. Max could feel him watching.

Max looked into the dive hole and shivered. He glanced back at Andre. "I'm sorry. I meant it when I said I want your help."

Andre smiled, his hands shoved deep in his pockets. "Good."

"I know my mood is going to get worse. I can be a real asshole. I'd better say this now." Max took a deep breath of cool air and a step toward Andre. "It's been a really crappy summer, one of the worst. But that one night with you…it was good, really good."

Andre's smile grew. He stepped forward, wrapped his arms around Max, and pulled him into a soft kiss. "For me too."

Max leaned his forehead against Andre's. "Maybe we can do it again sometime?"

"Maybe." Andre chuckled. "That's what I wanted to talk with you about." He straightened and looked into Max's eyes. "I know that what happened to you in the military makes you nervous about this, and I'll respect whatever you want, but it would be easier if you were here as my lover than as my... I don't know what to call it."

"Patient?" Max looked into Andre's deep blue eyes. He shrugged. "What the hell? I already lost my job."

"Good." Andre kissed him lightly. "Now let's get to work. We need to set up this equipment before dinner."

* * *

"Where's Henrick?" Max asked as he eyed the bottle of wine being opened for dinner.

Andre handed him juice. "At Palmer Station. He's vowed never to dive again, and we lent him to the penguin researchers. They needed an extra pair of hands for a survey."

"We've got way too many divers this year anyway." It was the blonde woman again. Max vaguely remembered her checkout dive, competent if not graceful.

Max swigged the juice. It was cloyingly sweet, and he almost gagged. He glanced at Andre, who wore an expression of amused tolerance.

After dinner, Max was completely unprepared for the good-natured hooting and jeering that accompanied his departure from the dorm with Andre, pup tent and sleeping bags in tow.

"Christ," he muttered as he stomped behind Andre. "They're like sailors at a whorehouse."

Andre laughed. "I'm afraid privacy isn't abundant here. They're not a bad group, though."

Max shook his head. "Not what I'm used to."

Andre placed his mittened hand in Max's. "Even the Navy has changed, *mon chou*. They repealed Don't Ask, Don't Tell."

Max tried to imagine what an out life in his platoon would have been like. Nope. Couldn't picture it.

His head pounded, a dull beat like a pulse over his right eye, and his muscles kept twitching as he unfurled and set up the little tent while Andre arranged the inside. When Max crawled in, he found Andre sitting on one half of a double sleeping bag, untying his boots.

He grinned at Max. "Did you know there's a special bin in the cold-weather supply storage filled with doubles?"

Max sank down beside him and began undressing. "What would you have done if I'd refused to come out?"

He shrugged. "Slept in the dorm. I brought another single. But one of us would have been swamped alone in this big bag."

Max smiled. "They say it's warmer if you're naked."

Andre chuckled softly and wiggled out of his clothing.

Max slid in next to Andre, whose skin felt smooth and warm compared with the slippery, cold sleeping bag.

Turning on his side to face Max, Andre ran a hand along his cheek. "How are you?"

Max shrugged, inhaling the sweet smell of naked flesh. "My head hurts, and I feel like an idiot."

Andre's lips brushed lightly against Max's. "Do you mind if we make love now? You're probably not going to feel like it tomorrow."

"Don't bet on that." Max ran his hand through Andre's curls and deepened the kiss.

Max tried to abandon himself to the slip and suck of their tongues, but he kept losing the rhythm. He felt awkward, like a kid in his first kiss. Only not like he'd been with his first, a boy who moved into the neighborhood the spring Max was fifteen and back out again in the fall. All summer, the two of them had gotten drunk on cheap sweet wine, paying more attention to each other than to the straight porn they pretended to watch, working their way from jerking off together to fisting each other's cocks to blowjobs and eventually to kissing, every time sufficiently drunk that they could say they didn't remember. Except Max had, and it changed everything. Kissing Andre in the cold tent was a thousand times more awkward than that.

Max pulled away. "I don't know how to do this without a buzz on."

Andre traced his cheekbone with an elegant finger, and the touch sent a shiver down Max's spine. Andre whispered, "Relax. Your body knows."

Max puffed out air between pursed lips. A deep, rotten, terrifying shame welled in his belly. "What if I can't?"

Andre smiled, his finger trailing down Max's jaw, his nail scraping against the stubble. "You can, Max Conway. People make love sober all the time."

Max held up his hand. They both watched it shake. "I'm a fucking mess."

"I've been remembering what it's like to crave, myself." Andre drew his finger across Max's lower lip. "I haven't stopped fantasizing about you since I first saw you leaning against the bar, downing tequila shots. Everything about you shouted trouble, and yet I couldn't stay away."

He captured Max's trembling hand and brought it to his cock. Max's fingers curled around the shaft, as involuntary as a sea anemone wrapping itself around the finger of a prodding diver. He could feel engorged veins pulsing and stiffening Andre to rock hard.

Andre thrust slowly into Max's fist and whispered, "Can you feel how much I want you? It's crazy."

The tension broke in Max, and he leaned into Andre's kiss. Wind flapped the tent sides. Andre's tongue pressed into Max's mouth, and his lips were hot compared with the cold air. The nylon bag rustled as Andre rolled Max onto his back. Andre's weight anchored him, and Max opened to the kiss. Andre thrust his tongue deeper. Max let his hands drift to Andre's back. He felt uncertain and young and ridiculously self-conscious. Andre reached between them, and Max jumped as his hand cupped Max's balls. Max relaxed again at the gentleness of his touch. Another wave of shame swept through Max as he realized he was only half-hard. This never happened to him. Never. Ever. He was the slam-it-home kid. No matter how drunk, he always got it up. But now, thirty-some hours sober, his dick was a slug.

"It's okay," Andre whispered, his fingers making tantalizing circles across Max's balls and up his cock. "Take your time."

Meanwhile Andre's hard cock was fucking Max's hand with slow thrusts that made him wonder how it would feel inside him, a thought that sent blood rushing into his prick, pumping it full and hard in Andre's grip. Andre moaned and dropped his lips to Max's nipple, biting gently. Bolts of excitement coursed through Max, bringing him fully erect.

"Fuck me hard enough to forget," Max whispered, spreading his knees as Andre fell between them. Andre pulled back and looked at Max. His eyes, dark blue in the yellow light of the tent, scanned Max's. Whatever he saw there made him smile.

Andre rolled away, and while he rummaged in the pack, Max stared at the tent walls, which seemed to breathe with the wind. He felt cold and nervous without Andre's body against his. Max closed his eyes, listening to the rustle of Andre unwrapping a condom and the slurp of lube slathered on latex.

"Now." Max's whisper came out like a rasp.

He pulled his knees close to his chest to keep them from shaking. Andre came back, his thighs warming the backs of Max's own. Max opened his eyes as the tip of Andre's cock pressed into him. Andre's gaze was hot on Max, his hands bracing Max's hips, holding him steady like ballast. The pressure of Andre's cock brought Max back to the moment, and he focused on the man pushing into him. Max's chest expanded as Andre filled him. He breathed into the pressure, and his muscles relaxed as pain became pleasure. It seemed like his nerve endings were alive for the first time. His body hungered for Andre, his skin ached to be touched, his cock swelled in Andre's fist. He watched Andre surging into him, looking like an angel, his hair a dark halo, his eyes hot blue like the center of a flame. Max pulled his knees closer, wanting more, wanting deeper, his whole world centered on the in and out of Andre's cock.

The sound of their breathing filled the tent, drowning even the wind sweeping across the frozen landscape. Max imagined the dark ocean below them. He might never see it again, but this—this moment with Andre deep inside him and Max feeling more alive than he had with any other man—this was worth even that high price. As Andre fucked and stroked him, Max abandoned himself to the chaos whirling up from deep within, a dark wave that carried him as it crested, spilling with a cry into the sweet breath between them.

* * *

But by the next night, Max's stomach churned, and his head ached. Andre offered him candy, juice, and aspirin, held him close, and whispered in his ear. Max wasn't sure whether the words were English or French, and it didn't matter.

In the middle of the night, Max started thrashing his way out of the sleeping bag, restlessness careening through his muscles.

"What is it?" Andre sat up beside him.

Max started pulling on his clothes. "I gotta get out of here."

Andre nodded and reached for his first layer of clothing. "All right. Let's take a walk."

The sun sparkled off the snow. Max blinked into the stinging brightness, and the wind bit his face. Andre reached into the tent and produced two pairs of sunglasses and two fleece scarves. "Which direction, *mon ami*?"

Max looked around. On three sides of the frozen landscape, distant purple mountains spiked above the surface of ice, and in the other, the ocean lay somewhere at the end of a flat expanse. The day before, a lone penguin had waddled through camp, miles from his fellows and heading in the wrong direction. Max had laughed until Andre explained that it was a suicide mission. The disoriented penguin would walk and walk into the distance, farther and farther away from food and companionship, eventually to die a hard, lingering death. He glanced in the direction the penguin had gone and chose the opposite, toward the distant sea.

Their boots crunching on the snow and the flutter of wind in their parkas were the only sounds for a long time.

Andre broke the silence. "Where did you grow up?"

It seemed such an innocuous, first-date question that Max laughed. "Cicero, near Chicago. My dad was a cop."

"Do you still have family there?" Andre's hood rustled as he turned to Max.

Max nodded. Wind flapped his clothing. "My folks are dead. But as far as I know, my brother's there with his family."

"Phineas." Andre pulled his scarf tight around his chin. "You're not close?"

Max shook his head violently. "God, no. He takes after my dad. No time for fags."

They were silent a while longer, their breath steaming the air as they walked. "And your mother? Did she have time for you?"

Max concentrated on the sound of his boots breaking the snow crust. "Don't know. She died when I was young. But I doubt it. She was a drunk."

Andre spoke softly. Max could barely hear him over the wind. "How did she die?"

Max closed his eyes. It wasn't something he wanted to remember. Ever. "Suicide."

"Oh, I'm sorry." Andre touched his arm. Max nodded and stepped away.

They trudged on, unbroken white before them, a long line of footsteps on the snow behind. Max thought about childhood monsters. Annie claimed she tripped to heal the wounds, but Max had been looking for escape. He hoped to fuck that sobriety didn't mean he'd be stuck feeling all this crap forever.

"So how about you?" Max thrust the words out, wanting out of his own head.

"You want my story?" Andre clapped his hands together against the cold.

The wind was fucking icy. If Max had a heart, he'd turn them around and head back to the relative warmth of the pup tent, but the idea of returning to that confined space made his skin crawl. "Sure. I don't like mine."

Andre chuckled. Max turned to see him looking off toward Mount Erebus. "My father was a diplomat. We moved often. My mother, she was beautiful and a little self-absorbed."

"You grew up with money?" It felt like they could walk forever across this white desert and never get closer to the mountains or the edge of the ice.

"Yes. And nannies. And private schools. And social obligations, which I did not like." Andre hunched against the wind. "So I ran away. I was maybe thirteen when I left my first boarding school, sixteen when I left my last. I spent a few years on the street." He cut his eyes at Max. "Earning money however I could. Don't worry. I have been tested and tested and tested again. It is an obsession with me."

"And the drugs?" The sound of their footfalls and the wind almost swallowed Max's words.

"I stopped at nineteen. I was lucky because I was able to finish my education and eventually find a good job. And now"—he spread his hands, as if encompassing the continent—"I can come here to study how the climate is changing, how the ocean responds to this big change we're making by heating up the world. For me, learning is the most important thing. It's a good life."

Max looked at him. "Do you miss it?"

"Heroin?" At Max's nod, Andre continued. "There are still times I'd like to climb out of my life, but all I have to do is remember how it was and compare that with now, and no, I don't miss it."

Max gazed at the man walking beside him and tried to imagine him as a jittery kid in need of a fix. But the image wouldn't gel. If his head would stop hurting for a minute, maybe he could figure that out. In the meantime, he walked, and Andre stayed beside him. If they kept going, eventually they were bound to end up somewhere.

Part Three

Ice Time

"Everyone is a visitor in Antarctica—no one lives there permanently—but there's always a shifting crew of scientists around doing research. That's because the continent, with its icy oceans, frigid temperatures, and unusual biology and geology, is like nowhere else on earth."

—Ice Stories: Dispatches from Polar Scientists

http://icestories.exploratorium.edu/dispatches/big-ideas/mcmurdo/

Chapter Thirteen

Breathing the thick smell wafting in from the lilac bush outside the open window, Max pressed the phone to his ear. Christ, what was he shaking for? It was only a job, and he'd never had trouble finding work. But this could never be just a job because Antarctica would always be there in his dreams.

"You're sober?" Chief Jackson's voice thundered through the phone. Strange to think it had been six months, the sun was gone from Antarctica, and that the chief was speaking out of that frozen darkness while Max basked in the Northern California afternoon sun.

Was he sober? He'd spent ninety days in a clinic north of Sacramento obsessively walking the grounds, sucking hard candies, biting his nails, rehashing his whole goddamned military career with a therapist, and telling complete fucking strangers his life story, and another ninety going to meetings, sometimes with Andre, sometimes alone, seeing a counselor at the VA, and picking up whatever one-day jobs he could find that wouldn't put him anywhere near a drink. He made a meeting a day, called his sponsor every night, and tried to forget the bite of tequila, the smooth, sweet taste of scotch, and the whisper of vodka. And most of the time it worked. So yeah, he was fucking sober.

"Yes, sir." He pressed a hand against his forehead, willing away the waves of shame that always waited, one wrong word away. People told him it would pass, but holy shit, was he ready to feel like a man again.

Chief Jackson let Max sweat for a few moments before he spoke. "Fax me a certificate from that recovery center you say you were in. And you'll be pissing in a jar every other goddamned minute."

"Yes, sir." Max twisted and re-twisted the rough drapery fabric, hope blooming in his chest. Maybe he could let himself remember what it felt like to float in that deep blue peace.

The chief paused again. Max watched a sparrow light on an oak in the neighbor's yard. "That professor of yours coming down with you this year?"

He looked toward the kitchen where he could hear pots banging. "Um, yes, sir."

"Good. I like him. He's got guts." Max could almost smell the coffee as the chief slurped in his ear. "You know, I don't care who you sleep with. Never did."

He blinked. "I…um… Thank you, sir."

"You think I didn't know why you left the SEALs? Boneheads. You're a fine diver. When you're sober." Chief Jackson's voice rumbled in Max's ear. "If you come back down, you'll have some apologies to make, I can tell you that."

"How is she?" He closed his eyes. Over the past few months he'd torn up every letter he'd started. Talking to Annie was the most important and hardest thing he could imagine doing.

Chief Jackson paused. "She's Annie. Better off without all that hippie-dippy-trippy stuff, if you ask me. But of course, you never did. She's into snow globes these days. You might want to bring one with you."

The sparrow flew away. Max bit his lip. "Yes, sir. Thank you, sir. You won't regret this."

Jackson chuckled. "Yes, I will. And probably every day. I warn you, first failed piss test and you're on a plane outta here."

"Yes, sir." Max stood and paced across the living room.

He crossed the kitchen threshold as the chief growled, "Stop sounding like a whipped dog, SEAL pup. It'll be good to have you back, son."

Andre looked up from the mound of beans he was chopping, his eyebrows an elegant arch.

Max signed off and wrapped his arms around Andre, visions of cold blue water cascading through his head.

* * *

Annie didn't meet the plane, she wasn't there for lunch, and she didn't peek in on orientation. Max slung his duffel onto the bed across from Andre's and considered his lover in the bright light of their small, dorm-like double. The room, unused all winter, smelled of dust and neglect. Max left the door open to air.

Andre smiled up from his bed where he lay sprawled out, watching Max. "How do you feel?"

Max tried to find a smile for him. "I'll live."

There was a knock at the open doorway. Bones leaned against the door frame, his familiar bulk clad in a tee with the outline of a diver drawn above the giant letters MUFF. He nodded to Andre and scowled at Max.

Smitty peered in from behind Bones, his face pinched. "Chief wants us in his office yesterday."

Max glanced at Andre, who shrugged and said, "I need to get the students sorted out. That young Kristin's going to be difficult. Try not to let her kill herself during Happy Camper, will you?"

Bones rolled his eyes. "Not another one. That German of yours was a fucking train wreck."

Andre gave a very French shoulder roll. "I screened this one for claustrophobia."

Max grabbed his parka and followed Bones and Smitty into the brightly lit hallway.

As they passed the dorm lounge, which smelled disconcertingly of stale beer, Bones cleared his throat. "Are you and the professor...?"

Max gave him a look. "You got a problem with that?"

Bones shook his head, slamming through the doorway into the dorm foyer. "You mean other than it makes me wanna puke? And for the record, it sucks that you played us, pretending you were all real man when you're a fucking shit packer."

Max stopped. His hands curled into fists. "You need me to prove my manhood to you now? As I remember, the last time we went a few rounds you couldn't dive for days."

Bones shrugged into his parka. "So what if you can fight. That don't make cocksucking right."

Max turned to Smitty. "How about you? You agree with Bonair?"

Smitty looked down at the scuffed gray carpeting, toying with his coat hem. "Shit, man. You gotta understand how much this creeps us out. I mean, you've seen me naked. How do I know you weren't jerking off thinking about it later?"

Max snorted, his whole body tense. "Don't flatter yourself."

Smitty pushed an arm into the sleeve of his parka. "We better move along before the chief fires us."

Max stepped back to let them pass through the doorway ahead of him. Fucking divers. Maybe it was easier this way. At least he wouldn't be tempted to go out drinking with them. Not that he could remember why he'd wanted to in the first place.

They walked in silence across the frozen McMurdo mud.

* * *

Max stood outside Annie's door. He heard soft music. He raised his hand to knock and paused, listening to his heart pounding in his ears. He hit the door with three quick taps.

Rustling from inside, and the door opened. Annie stood before him in an oversized tee and dark blue pajama pants decorated with moons and stars. She blinked up at him, her face stiff. "I heard you were arriving today."

He gazed down at her. He could almost hear the gurgle of his heart filling up. "Hey, Annie. I'm really sorry."

She nodded and stepped back to let him in. The room looked the same, except for the blank spots above and under the spare bed. The faint scent of patchouli made Max's chest ache.

He gestured toward the empty bed. "You managed to keep the room a single?"

She shrugged. "Same roommate. She won't show up until mainbody, and after that she'll be out at the pole most of the time."

"That's good." He shuffled from one foot to the other, trying to remember the speech he'd practiced.

Annie didn't sit and didn't offer him a seat. She looked up at him impassively. "You fucked up big-time, Mac."

Max swallowed. "I know. I'd do anything to be able to undo it. I thought I wouldn't betray your trust for the world, and yet I did."

She nodded and gestured for him to sit on the spare bed. Folding herself onto her own bed, she considered him. "Jackson says you quit drinking."

He perched on the edge of his old bed. "Six months now."

"Good." She picked at a loose thread in her coverlet. "Thanks for running after me. Everyone says you were a fucking maniac."

Max's shoulders relaxed a little. "No sweat."

She bit her lip, a habit that always elongated the unscarred side of her face. "And thanks for getting rid of the acid. I would have been in a world of hurt if you hadn't."

He exhaled. "Wish I could take credit for that, but it was Andre's idea."

The edge of her mouth tipped up. "You're all out and proud now?"

Max leaned forward, propping his elbows on his knees. "Out, I guess. Still working on proud. Working on being someone I can be proud of."

She considered him. "You ever drink again, I'm outta this friendship for good. You got it?"

He smiled. "Does that mean you're in it now?"

She shrugged. "None of us are perfect, Mac. But I can't believe you didn't write or anything all winter."

He looked at his shoes. "Would you believe I did? I tore up the letters and deleted the e-mails before I could send them. Didn't know how you'd react. I mean, you had a right to hate me."

She shook her head. "How could I hate you? You're my best friend."

Max stood. He reached into the kangaroo pocket of his hoodie and brought out a small box. "I brought you this."

Annie's eyebrows rose. "It's not drugs, is it? I'm off those for good."

Max shook his head and held out the package. She unwrapped it, reached into the box, and pulled out the snow globe with a red and yellow surfer scene. Annie shook it, dislodging the silver sparkles meant to look like water droplets spewing from crashing waves.

She laughed. "That is the tackiest thing I've ever seen."

Max grinned. "I knew you'd like it. I figured if the girl can't get to the beach, I should bring the beach to her."

Annie stood and opened her arms. "It's good to see you, Mac."

He hugged her back. "Annie, you're the best."

* * *

When Max got back to the room, Andre had pushed a bureau out of the way and pressed the twin beds together in one corner of the room. Max paused in the doorway, stopped by a shot of adrenaline. It didn't get more in-your-face gay than this. Andre looked up from tucking in a bedsheet. He smiled, and Max's heart slowed. It didn't matter what anyone else thought. Max had a job he loved and a lover worth going through hell for.

Andre wiggled his eyebrows. "We have an hour before dinner. Do you want to try out our new bed?"

Max kicked the door closed behind him and stepped into Andre's arms. He inhaled the spicy scent of Andre mixed with the familiar McMurdo musk. Same place, same smells, same man as the summer before, but everything felt different. Andre's tongue tangling with Max's tasted like home. They broke, stripped, and fell together onto the bed, their skin familiar silk. The bed creaked as Andre rolled, bringing Max on top. Andre wrapped his legs around Max's back, his fingers digging into the flesh of his ass. Max rocked against him, their cocks caressing. He buried himself in the kiss, one hand braced against the bed, the other stroking the stubble along Andre's jaw.

Andre moaned beneath him and reached for the lube. They'd both been tested and stopped using condoms months before. He slicked Max before looping his legs over Max's shoulders and pressing his ass against his cock. Max pushed in, pausing for a few seconds as Andre's jaw tightened, thrusting deep when he relaxed. Andre clamped tight and hot around him as he drove in. Andre panted and flushed. Sweat trickled down Max's spine as he brought his hand to fist Andre's cock.

He watched as Andre closed his eyes and writhed, his mouth open and long neck arching, so beautiful that it made Max's heart ache. He saw Andre's orgasm coming in the curl of his tongue and the flutter of his eyelids, and he pounded harder, moving his hips and hand in rhythm as the pulse of it crashed over him, into and through Andre, in wave after wave, until he felt both emptied and filled.

As Max pulled out, Andre drew him close, wrapping his arms around Max like a blanket. The long day fell away as Max drifted into a dream of cool blue water beneath an icy sky.

* * *

There was only one building on McMurdo where Max had never been—the Chapel of the Snows. It sat at the end of town, looking like a cardboard cutout from a 1950's Christmas card, complete with arched stained glass windows and a bell tower.

"I feel like an idiot." Max muttered, one foot on the front step. From where he stood, he could see both McMurdo bars.

Beside him, Andre stopped. "Meetings are the same everywhere, *mon cher*."

Max grunted. "Except anonymous isn't part of the McMurdo vocabulary."

"You want to turn back, we can turn back." Andre rested his hand on Max's arm. "There's always next week."

Max looked into those deep blue eyes. Andre was serious. He'd skip it for Max, even though he had to be wanting a meeting himself since back home he went to

two or three every week. Andre's bottomless patience—
it always worked. How did he know that the best way to
get Max to take his own recovery seriously was to give
him permission to fail. *If you don't mind, it don't matter.*
Max took a deep breath, climbed the three steps and
opened the chapel door.

The main chapel was a long well-lit room where
several rows of chairs faced a pulpit. Stars were visible
through a large window at the front. Over the past six
months, Max had been in plenty of church basements
but never the sanctuary. He still wasn't comfortable with
that whole higher power thing, but the chapel had a
comfortable, lived in, very McMurdo feel to it and he
started to relax. Laughter came from an alcove. When
he first started going to meetings, the laughter had
baffled him—what did a bunch of people who couldn't
drink anymore have to laugh about? But now he was
used to it. And in California, every so often he had
found himself joining in.

A half dozen people looked up as they entered
the alcove. The only one he recognized was one of the
dishwashers from the year before. With a huge smile,
she jumped up and embraced Andre.

"I was starting to think no one from the old
group would show this year."

Andre squeezed her back. "Great to see you.

How's your daughter?"

She dug in her purse and produced a photo. "She had it right after I got off ice--a baby boy with all ten toes and fingers."

While Andre pored over the photo and made all the appropriate baby appreciation noises, one of the men smiled at Max and gestured toward an empty chair. Max sat and shook hands with him, and the man sitting next to him and the woman beside him and so on, until he'd been greeted by them all. He told himself that this was just another meeting, like any of the hundred or so that he'd been to in the past six months. Andre smiled at Max as he slid into the chair next to him. He brushed Max's arm. Max fought the urge to jerk away. His first instinct was always to hide their relationship but what was the point? Everyone knew everything on McMurdo. Besides, it was time he quit keeping secrets. If anyone had an issue with his sexuality, well, fuck them. He straightened. Out and proud, like Annie had said. If you don't mind, *they* don't matter.

The dishwashing grandmother cleared her throat. "Welcome to the Ross Island AA group." She smiled at Andre. "Since as far as we know, this is the only twelve step meeting on the continent, we welcome anyone in recovery, no matter what your drink or drug of choice. Let's go around the room and introduce ourselves."

The words were familiar. Max relaxed a little more.

Beside him Andre said, "Hello everyone. My name is Andre and I'm a grateful recovering addict." He looked at Max. "And today there's a lot for which to be grateful."

Max held his gaze while the group greeted him. What the fuck did Max care what anyone else thought? It was his own fucking life. He turned back to the group. "Max, alcoholic."

"Hi, Max." A warm, welcoming sound.

And then the attention moved on to the next guy. Max looked around the circle. The last time he'd been on the ice he'd had two drinking buddies and one friend who really knew him. This year would be better. He looked at Andre. The best yet.

* * *

Sliding through the McMurdo mud, Max followed Andre to the edge of town, where a trail led to Observation Hill. They trudged through the waning gray daylight, the sounds and smells of diesel trucks fading the farther they walked from the station. Bright orange and gold streaks appeared on the horizon as sunset took over the sky. In the distance, Max could make out the silhouette of Mount Erebus, backlit by the setting sun. The quiet grew. Their boots squeaked in the snow, and thighs swished in survival suits. Max loved the way Andre moved as he walked ahead on the path. How Andre managed to look graceful geared up in an orange survival suit and black backpack was beyond Max. Maybe it was because Max knew how the muscles rippled underneath all those clothes.

The light disappeared as they neared the peak. Andre swung the pack off his back and produced a survival blanket, which he spread on the snow. In the dark, Max could make out the gleam of his eyes peering from his balaclava.

"It's crazy having a picnic in the dark at thirty below," Max muttered, fumbling in his own backpack and bringing out the thermos of hot tea he'd procured from the kitchen.

Andre chuckled. "It is. You're right. But look how beautiful our station is from here." He gestured toward the tumble of lights below, the oil tanks laid out like thick silver buttons. Flopping onto the blanket, he pointed toward the sky. "And have you ever seen anything so beautiful as this?"

Max looked down at him. "Yeah, I have."

Andre smiled. "You're trying to flatter me?"

Max sat beside him, patting his knee through the thick layers of fabric. "No flattery, just fact." He leaned back and gazed into the sky, the stars so thick they looked painted. "But you're right. This is amazing."

They lay together, enjoying the glorious sky.

Andre rolled onto his side. His head loomed over Max's, dark except for the skin around his eyes. "Are you happy to be back?"

Max brushed his mitten over Andre's shoulder. "Yes. I wasn't sure how I was going to get over it if I never saw Antarctica again. And it's better because I'm here with you." He took a deep breath. "In treatment they kept hounding us about how we needed to talk about our feelings. It isn't easy."

"I know." Andre's breath fogged the space between them.

Max looked away, watching the stars and thinking of all the possible worlds in the universe. He turned back to Andre. "I should have said this before. Long before, I guess. But I kept thinking you'd know without my saying it." He laughed. "You'd think I'd have told someone this before, but I haven't."

Andre cocked an eyebrow.

Max gazed into his beautiful eyes. "I love you."

"I know." Andre brushed his lips against Max's, a muffled kiss blocked by the balaclava. "I love you too."

The wind blew Andre's hood against his cheek. Max sighed. "This would be really romantic if it wasn't for all these clothes and the cold."

Andre chuckled. "There may be a flaw in my plan. Shall we go home?"

Max nodded. "Lead on, baby. I'll be right behind you."

"That sounds like a good time." Andre sat and started packing up. "How about a picnic in bed?"

Max laughed. He took a deep breath of cold air and sky and snow. The temperature was thirty below, but tonight would be a warm night in Antarctica.

The end

by Dev Bentham

Chapter One

I wrote on the board, *The first rule of ecology is that small shifts beget big change.*

Under that I added, *Everything is connected.*

Communicating my love of science to students was the best part of my job. I love interacting with all those fresh minds eager to change the world. But I hated the awkwardness of the first day of class. When I first started teaching, I was about five years older than most of my students. I felt connected to them—we were the same generation. But each year the students seemed to get younger. Fifteen years later that feeling of connection didn't happen on the first day, or even in the first week. With most of the students, I still got there eventually, but every year it took more work.

Isaac sat in the back row, third seat from the window. Sunlight streamed through the glass forming a golden finger that landed like a caress on his chiseled cheekk. Most of the other students I recognized, having passed them in the hallway from time to time as they stumbled through their first years here. Many of my colleagues developed close relationships with the students, watching them grow through four, and sometimes five, years of the expensive education their parents were providing. I, on the other hand, only had them in one course, a class sufficiently physically and intellectually grueling that I was sure they were grateful that one course was all they had to take from me. But I did take note of them as they passed my office in small, chatty clusters or single, preoccupied strolls.

And I certainly would have noticed Isaac with his dark curls and elegant stride, so different from the beefy men and outdoorsy women who normally peopled my world. Students at Saint Genevieve's, a small Catholic college in the suburbs of Chicago, tended to clomp around campus in ragged jeans and thick, plaid wool shirts. Among these dandelions, Isaac, with his tight dark jeans, long-sleeved tees, and strong Jewish profile, stuck out like a lily. My first thought on seeing him was, wouldn't my mama be proud if I brought home such a nice Jewish boy? My second was, are you out of your frigging mind?

I was neither out nor in at school, simply a single, perpetual bachelor academic. I'd let it be known that my previous relationships did not pan out, mostly because of work. My colleagues understood. Their own marriages and

entanglements suffered from the seventy-hour workload
we shouldered each week in order to teach and research the
subjects about which we were most passionate. It might not
have surprised most of them, and I wouldn't have lost my job,
if I let it be known that the person who moved out a few years
ago was named Bill. Jenny Karn, our marvelous microbiologist,
brought Leslie with her to all department functions. But I did
know, very well, the passage in the morals clause I signed, the
one that related to schtupping students. It was grounds for
dismissal, no matter their gender.

And so I looked at everyone but Isaac Wolf as I lectured
that fine September morning. But I can't remember anyone
else who was there.

* * * *

I dismissed the students with only minutes to go before
the Friday faculty meeting. Our chair, a chemist named
Geoffrey Dunn, insisted that four on Friday was the only time
when everyone was free to meet. Never mind that Wednesdays
at eight in the morning were equally free, that several faculty
members had children who needed to be picked up from
school or day care in the late afternoon, or that by late Friday
everyone was in a foul mood. The time suited Geoffrey.

I sprinted across campus to the library. We met in a
conference room buried in the bowels of the old rambling
building. I padded through the stacks, passing students
already engaged in research—or cruising each other amidst
the books. The conference room door was closed, meaning
Geoffrey had started without me. No surprise. I wasn't one of

his favorite colleagues. I could never tell if it was some sort of unconscious homophobia or that I challenged him whenever he was spectacularly wrong. Or maybe he simply didn't like me.

I didn't like him either. Geoffrey wanted to destroy my course—the only class I taught, a yearlong survey of ecological sampling techniques that was required for students in the natural resources program. Saint Genevieve's had a surprisingly good history of placing students in the few natural resources jobs available to undergraduates and an astonishingly high rate of acceptance for graduate programs in the field. I liked to think it was because of my course. Years later I heard from students that mine was the course that changed their lives.

That was what kept me teaching.

Geoffrey Dunn and his faculty meetings were not. I anticipated his glare as I opened the door.

Geoffrey chose to ignore me as I slipped into the vacant chair beside Jenny. She smiled and passed me an agenda. I skimmed the contents.

"Are we going to battle this crap again?" I muttered under my breath to her, pointing to the fifth item on the agenda.

She gave me a sympathetic glance.

For five years running, Geoffrey had proposed we change the requirements for the major. He had a few scattered suggestions here and there, but the big one was to turn my sixteen-credit methods course into an elective, which would cut its enrollment in half. The inevitable result would be that

the course would shift to an every-other-year schedule, and I'd
be left to teach everyone else's leftovers on the off years. Not to
mention that half our graduates would be flung into the world
with no practical skills.

I was tired of the debate and could have argued both
sides in my sleep. Geoffrey would contend that my course
was too hard, that I drove students away from the program
and kept them from taking other courses, most notably his
own favorite, which was periodically canceled due to low
enrollment. I would argue that while students came into my
course seeing it as a grade point killer, by the end of the year
most of them were happy with the marketable skills they'd
learned. It was the last chance students got to learn techniques
they'd need for a career in natural resource management. Sure,
I demanded a lot. Our fragile planet's future was in their
sweaty palms. Sometimes that scared me to death. Sometimes
it made me hopeful.

So far my colleagues had agreed with me. At some
point the politics might shift toward him. I wasn't sure what
I'd do then. Resign in a fit of pique or meekly acquiesce to
teach whatever crumbs he gave me? Whichever way the wind
was going to blow, I wasn't up to the debate this early in the
year, and let a few other faculty argue in favor of keeping my
course. Geoffrey and his cronies said their predictable bits, and
eventually the question was tabled and the meeting droned
on. My course had survived another meeting.

After adjournment, I turned to Jenny as she gathered
her belongings. "Hey, do you know a student named Isaac
Wolf? He's in my capstone class."

Her face split into a wide smile. "Isaac? He's a great kid. Really smart. You'll like having him in class."

I scraped back my chair, getting ready to stand. "I don't think I've seen him around before."

She stood. "He took a couple of years off. He stopped by my office last week. I'm not surprised you didn't recognize him. He's grown out his hair and gotten rid of the glasses. Slimmed down some too."

I nodded. "That would explain it."

"How's the research going?" Jenny asked as we made our way out of the room.

"Very well, actually. I signed three new clients over the summer. We should have plenty to do this winter." In addition to my own work on Bioindicators—the aquatic organisms who act as canaries in the coal mines for polluted waterways—I ran a small business identifying worms and insects sent to me by state agencies and other researchers interested in quantifying the extent of impact a given pollution event has had on their water body. The funds generated supported student workers and bought necessary equipment, and I got a great deal of personal satisfaction from the work. None of which eased the essential loneliness of my life. But it helped pass the time.

* * * *

I hated the Friday faculty meetings, but, invariably, halfway home I'd be wishing I was still there. It had been almost three years, but ever since Bill left, the apartment, already small, seemed to cave in on me. I didn't pretend we'd had a good relationship and I probably should have felt relief when he went. Instead I was angry. I'd put up with a lot—his jokes about how dry and boring I was, his drinking, the other men and watching the clock tick by on a Saturday night wondering if he would decide to come home. What had I gotten in return? A burning urethra, ten days of antibiotics, and a bone deep fear that lasted for months while I had myself tested and tested and re-tested until I could be sure I was clean.

Now I was over him. The air no longer vibrated with my unresolved anger. But I had once thought I'd loved Bill and I still missed having someone I could care about more than I cared about work or the state of the world or even myself. Alone, all those things filled the apartment until it was hard to breathe. I stayed away as much as possible, eating in restaurants, visiting my mother, grading in coffee shops, working in my lab until I was tired enough to fall asleep without dreaming. I couldn't wait to be back in the classroom on Monday.

* * * *

One Monday, Isaac looked up at me from under those impossibly long lashes, his smile slow and sexy, as I dropped the nearly perfect, graded midterm on his desk. The night before I'd added *brilliant* to the growing list of adjectives strung in my head beside his name. Which didn't help. Smart was sexy. And in the morning, I'd woken from a dream so vivid I was surprised to find myself alone. My lips tingled with the fantasy of his beautiful collarbone beneath them. Now I looked down at that same spot peeking from beneath his unbuttoned stark white shirt. For a moment I stood mesmerized by his cider-colored skin against the white.

My eyes met his for an instant. Every year at least a couple of the young women flirted with me, usually shyly, but occasionally more overtly. Once before I'd had a male student awkwardly express his interest. But this was different. Every cell in my body was on high alert. Isaac's half smile and the hot brown light of his eyes let me know I'd been discovered. He knew I wanted him. The shift in power between teacher and student was palpable.

I gave the briefest of nods. "Well done, Mr. Wolf."

Isaac's smile widened. "Thank you, Dr. Kohn."

His smile and the promise it contained followed me around the room as I delivered the bad news of the first graded test. It left my heart pounding, whether from terror or anticipation, I couldn't tell.

Learning from Isaac
by Dev Bentham

from Love is a Light Press
Look for it on Amazon and Barnes and Noble

Dev Bentham

Dev Bentham writes soulful m/m romance. Her characters are flawed and damaged adult men who may not even know what they are missing, but whose lives are transformed by true love.

Love is a Light Titles by Dev Bentham

August Ice

* * * *

The TARNISHED SOULS Series
Learning from Isaac
Fields of Gold

Coming soon to Love is a Light:
Sacred Hearts
Bread, Salt and Wine

Other books by Dev
Driving into the Sun
Nobody's Home
Painting in the Rain
Moving in Rhythm